DAUGHTER OF THE ALIEN WARRIOR

TREASURED BY THE ALIEN 3

HONEY PHILLIPS

BEX MCLYNN

Copyright © 2020 by Honey Phillips and Bex McLynn

All rights reserved. No part of this book may be used or reproduced by any means, graphic, electronic, or mechanical, including photocopying, recording, taping or by any information storage retrieval system without the written permission of the author.

Disclaimer
This book is a work of fiction. Names, characters, places, and incidents are products of the author's imagination or are used fictitiously and are not to be construed as real. Any resemblance to actual events, locales, organizations, or people, living or dead, is entirely coincidental.

Cover Design by Cameron Kamenicky and Naomi Lucas
Edited by Lindsay York at LY Publishing Services

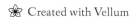 Created with Vellum

CHAPTER ONE

Jade reached out and turned off the 5:00 a.m. alarm before it could ring. She hadn't been sleeping; she rarely did anymore. Instead, she dragged herself out of bed and started her morning routine. Fifteen minutes of strength training, thirty minutes on the treadmill—her daughter's name echoing in her head with every step—and a final fifteen minutes of yoga, practiced for control rather than the serenity she had lost.

After a quick shower, she pulled on black yoga pants, a sports bra, and tank, then tucked her short dark hair under a matching black hoodie. As she moved along the upstairs hallway in the huge empty house, past the bedrooms she had once hoped to fill, she paused at the door to her daughter's room. Her eyes went to the empty crib as they did every morning.

I'm going to find you, baby.

The coffeemaker finished brewing as she arrived in the kitchen. She filled up the waiting thermos, grabbed a protein bar that she would have to force herself to eat, and headed for her big black Escalade. The last thing she did before she left the house was strap on her gun.

As she pulled out of the driveway, the car clock read 6:15.

When she arrived at the city park, the parking area was empty. Good. That meant no one was in danger. She parked at one end of the lot and took a sip of coffee as the sky began to lighten. In earlier years, she would have enjoyed the sight, but her husband was dead and her daughter was missing and there was no joy left in her world.

As she got out of the car to begin her rounds, she paused. The air was still, not even a whisper of birdsong breaking the silence. The hair on her neck stood up, and then she smiled. Perhaps today her hunt would be rewarded. Slipping into the edge of the woods next to the walking trail, she waited.

Ten minutes later, two minivans pulled into the parking lot. Ashley and Naomi always walked on Wednesday mornings. They were both young, pretty. *Trophy wives*, she thought dispassionately as she watched them pull out the latest model jogging strollers and buckle in their babies. Normally, they chattered and laughed like the missing birds, but today, the oppressive silence seemed to be affecting them as well.

After a short discussion and several nervous looks around, they headed down the sidewalk. They liked to take the long way around and come back by the lake. She followed them silently, determined not to let them out of her sight.

They kept a brisk pace, darting nervous glances around, but there was only the silent park and Jade slipping along behind them, unobserved. By the time they reached the lake meadow, they were almost jogging, anxious to get back to their cars. The mist off the lake was even thicker than normal, cloaking the area in white shadows, and Jade closed in, no longer worried about being seen.

A muffled cry came from in front of her and she ran, arriving in time to see a man in a black suit bending down over one of the women while another reached for the stroller.

"No!" she yelled. "You're not taking another baby."

She pulled out her gun and flicked off the safety. The year of training was about to pay off.

"Put the baby down and back away."

The barest whisper of sound came from behind her, and then there was a hand over hers as long, cold fingers, too many fingers, tried to wrestle the gun from her grip. She instinctively clenched her hand, determined not to lose the weapon, and there was a loud bang. Before she had time to register the shot, a sharp pain bit into her neck. The gun dropped from her limp fingers as the world started to spin. The last thing she saw before she descended into darkness was Ashley and Naomi floating away across the meadow.

As Jade struggled back to consciousness, she reached instinctively for her gun but found only the empty holster. Fuck. That wasn't good. The last thing she remembered was being by the lake. What happened to her?

Her head ached and there was a lingering pain in her shoulder, but she didn't sense any other injuries. Keeping her eyes closed, she tried to use her other senses to gather information about her surroundings. The air was cool and dry with a slight medicinal odor. She heard a faint sob, and then a minute later, a baby cried. A sudden, wild hope filled her heart. Could it be...?

Her eyes sprang open and she sat up, her hand still clutching the empty holster. Disappointment washed over her as she saw Ashley cradling her baby, trying desperately to quiet her as she shot a nervous look behind Jade. Of course. It would have been foolish to assume the kidnappers took her directly to her daughter. But perhaps she was one step closer. She surveyed her surroundings anxiously, looking for any clue as to her whereabouts.

Both she and Ashley were perched on narrow cots. Naomi sprawled on a third one, her son tucked in her arms, both of them sleeping. Clear plastic containers floated next to each cot, and white metal walls formed three sides of the room. The fourth wall consisted of a single glass panel and on the other side of the glass were two men in black suits. Or rather, two beings...

As she studied them closer, she realized that they were most definitely not men. Matte black hair topped skin as white as if they had applied the thick makeup her grandmother had worn on ceremonial occasions. But this wasn't makeup, and her sobo never had glowing red eyes or six fingers on each hand.

Their presence, combined with the metal walls and the banks of strange-looking equipment in the corridor behind them, led to only one impossible conclusion. *Aliens.* Her daughter had been taken by aliens. No wonder the police she had hounded constantly and the leagues of private detectives she had hired were unable to find a trace of Hana.

Her initial dismay—she now had an entire universe to search—was replaced by determination. She was closer to her daughter now than she had been for the past year.

"Kwaret appears to be correct. The product is less troublesome when stored with the breeders," one of the aliens said begrudgingly.

Although she could hear a faint clicking noise beneath their words, she understood them perfectly. Good. Hopefully, that meant they would also understand her. She rose and went to the panel, ignoring how weak her legs felt.

"I'm looking for my daughter. You took her a year ago. Where is she now?"

The alien who had spoken gave her a disinterested look, then ignored her and turned back to his companion.

"I'm not as sure about his suggestion to provide all of them with translators. I have no desire to hear slaves address me."

Slaves?

"His argument is that it will make it easier to have them obey our commands."

"I've always found a shock collar to be an effective training tool."

"But it also causes damage, and they fetch a higher price when they are undamaged."

If they thought she was going to obey some strange alien's commands, they had another think coming. She smacked her hand against the glass, smiling when one of them jumped.

"I said I'm looking for my daughter. Where is she?"

"Breeders are to be seen and not heard," the alien said disdainfully.

Her fist clenched, longing to smack that supercilious look off his face.

"Breeder?" the other alien asked.

"If she is looking for a child, then she must have produced one." He scanned her again, sneering. "Although I admit she looks to be past her prime breeding years. Still, a fertile female is worth more than a non-fertile one. Commander Kadica will be pleased with the potential for extra profit."

Fertile? She bit back a derisive retort. It had taken ten years and hundreds of thousands of dollars before she had been able to become pregnant.

"You mean you hope he will forgive you for bringing her on board rather than eliminating her."

The two males exchanged a nervous glance.

"If you two assholes won't listen to me, take me to your commander," she demanded.

"You would be well served if I did so." His hand went to a small box attached to his belt, but the other alien reached out and stopped him.

"Kragan, you can't do that. You know his temper. If she shows no more respect than she has done so far, he will punish her. If she's lucky enough to live through it, she would be too damaged to bring in more than a modest amount of credits. We only have the five of them to sell this time and I want to get as much profit from this trip as I can."

Kragan's hand dropped away. "I suppose you're right. The more credits we bring this trip, the more sponsors we will have for the next one."

The next one? Jade stared after them in distress as the two aliens turned and walked away. They had to be stopped. No other woman should have to face the pain she had lived with this past year.

"Ash? What's going on?" Naomi's sleepy voice sounded behind her, and she turned to find the other woman sitting up on her cot.

"I don't know!" Ashley wailed. She was a pretty, petite blonde with big blue eyes and a helpless air. "We were in the park and then I woke up here and there are these creepy men and I don't like it. I want to go home!" She burst into tears.

It didn't surprise Jade that Naomi was made of sterner stuff. A statuesque redhead with a sharp brain behind a seductive smile, she immediately focused on Jade.

"Who are you? Do you know what's going on?"

"You probably won't believe me, but we've been captured by aliens."

"What the fuck?" Naomi stared at her with obvious skepticism.

Jade had followed these two every Wednesday for the past four months and she knew all about them, including Naomi's past as a Las Vegas showgirl and her cynical view of the world. She hadn't expected to convince her.

"I know it sounds crazy, but you'll see for yourself soon enough."

"Why? What do they want from us?"

"They called us breeders," Ashley sobbed.

Naomi's eyes narrowed. "In other words, they're like every other bastard male out there."

"Not exactly," Jade said dryly.

The woman looked down at her admittedly impressive body. "If they're males, I can handle them."

Jade suspected that wouldn't prove to be true with these aliens, but she didn't argue. At that moment, Ashley's daughter, Heather, began to cry again.

"She's hungry." Ashley looked around frantically. "Did they bring her diaper bag? She needs a bottle. And a diaper change," she added, screwing up her nose.

The crying baby woke up Naomi's son, Justin, and he added to the noise. For the first time, the woman's nonchalant air cracked as she picked up her son and tried to comfort him.

"I can't stand it when he cries."

Jade's heart ached as she turned back to the front of the cell, pounding on the glass. She wouldn't care if Hana cried every day as long as she was with her again.

She beat a steady rhythm on the glass, yelling for Kragan, for the commander, for anyone to come and pay attention. Her hands were throbbing by the time another alien appeared. She didn't recognize this one and he approached with an almost deferential demeanor, unlike the arrogance of the other two.

"You must keep quiet," he said nervously. "You do not want to arouse the commander's wrath."

"The babies are hungry. I'm not going to be quiet until they are fed."

"I don't understand. Why don't their mothers feed them? That was my argument for placing them in the same cell with you."

She gave him an exasperated look. "They aren't being breastfed. That means they need bottles. Formula?"

"Oh dear. I didn't consider that."

"You don't have anything to feed them?" she asked in alarm, then switched to thinking about alternatives. "Do you have some type of cereal? Something that could make a very thin gruel? Or what about milk—something that animals feed to their young?"

He looked shocked. "I would never feed an infant anything like that."

"They have to be fed something," she said impatiently. "We have to try at least."

"No, no. You don't understand. I can provide a healthy formula. The, umm, bottles are a little more difficult but I will see what I can do."

Despite his words, he was already moving to the bank of equipment on the far side of the corridor. In a surprisingly short time, he returned bearing two odd-looking containers, but since they had nipples, she assumed they were intended as bottles.

Ashley and Naomi had joined her at the glass as they tried to comfort their crying children, and they eyed the alien with distrust.

"What's in there?" Ashley asked. "Heather is on a strictly

organic formula."

"Are there drugs in there? Are you giving them something just to shut them up?"

At Naomi's question, he looked horrified.

"Of course not. This formula is specially designed for human infants. They will thrive on it."

"How do you know that?" Jade asked, her heart racing. *I knew it!* These bastards had taken her daughter.

"You are not the first," he said evasively, opening the glass panel far enough to give the containers to the other women.

They took them reluctantly, glancing at them with suspicion before Naomi sighed and presented the makeshift bottle to her son. He latched on immediately. Ashley hesitated longer but she apparently couldn't resist her daughter's cries, and she too offered a bottle. Heather didn't seem concerned about whether the formula was organic, sucking greedily.

Jade turned back to the alien, her suspicions confirmed.

"Listen... what's your name?"

He looked oddly shy. "I am Kwaret."

"Listen, Kwaret, I knew there had to have been others. You took my daughter. I have to find her."

His eyes widened. "Your daughter? Why do you think I took her?"

"I don't mean you personally," she said. "Your... people. One of your ships was here a year ago."

Kwaret closed his eyes briefly, then admitted, "It is possible that a Vedeckian ship has been here before."

"I'm sure of it. How else could she have disappeared so completely? Do you know where she is?"

"I am not aware of any human children that are not with a family," he said slowly.

"What do you mean by family?" She gestured over at

Naomi and Ashley, both now sitting and feeding their children. "Do you mean they're with their mothers?"

He looked oddly thoughtful. "Are biological ties required to form a family?"

"You know what I mean," she snapped. "Did you sell human children to an alien family?"

The thought of her sweet daughter being sold like some type of pet made her throat close up.

He cast another look over his shoulder and closed his mouth.

Although Kwaret refused to answer any more questions, he told them how to use the clear plastic containers. They turned out to be a high-tech version of a crib. Not only did they provide a place for the babies to rest, but their padding also absorbed their waste and cleansed them. There was a small bathroom at the rear of the room for the women to use.

After he left, the three of them sat and stared at each other.

"Who are you?" Naomi asked again. "Were you jogging in the park?"

"No, I was following you."

"Why were you following us?" Ashley edged a little closer to Naomi. "Are you with them?"

A bitter laugh escaped. "No, but I was looking for them. It just never occurred to me that they would be aliens."

"I don't understand."

"My daughter disappeared from the same place a year ago. They killed my husband and they took her."

"Killed him?" Ashley's eyes widened. "Why didn't you tell us that we were in danger?"

"His death was in all the papers."

It had been a one-week wonder in the press, but longer for her when she fell under suspicion because she hadn't been with him. Instead, she had been foolishly clinging to a vestige of her pre-pregnancy life. At Nathan's insistence, she had been on a conference call with her Board of Directors when he was killed. It had been the only way he would consent to taking Hana for her walk and, in the vain hope that it might awaken some spark of fatherly feeling, she had agreed to his condition. She had lived with the guilt ever since.

"I assumed you knew about it." She tapped her empty holster ruefully. "And I thought I was capable of protecting you. I didn't count on aliens."

"You were using us as bait, weren't you?" Naomi's eyes narrowed.

She battled against another wave of guilt. "Not exactly. I go to the park every morning." She didn't mention that she had thought Ashley and Naomi were her best hopes of drawing out whoever had kidnapped her daughter.

"I don't understand. Why would Bob let me go somewhere where a murder was committed?" Ashley looked truly distressed.

Naomi only shrugged. "Because he wants you thin and fit?"

"Is that why Stefan let you go?"

"If it didn't affect the stock market, I doubt he even knew about it." Naomi shrugged again. "I knew what I was getting into when I married him. Didn't you know what Bob was like?"

"He's not like that!" Ashley cried as Naomi and Jade exchanged a disbelieving look.

Jade too had been married to a wealthy man whose main interest was his financial affairs, and as they had gotten older, she saw a number of first wives being traded in for younger models. She suspected that the only reason that Nathan hadn't done the same thing was because she owned a controlling interest in the company.

Naomi sighed and patted Ashley's back. "All right, sugar. If you say he's not like that, I'll believe you." She turned and looked at Jade. "So what do we do now?"

"We figure out how to get out of the cell and make these bastards take you and your children back to Earth."

"What about you?"

"I'm not going anywhere without my daughter."

CHAPTER TWO

Two weeks later...

"Remove your clothing," the Vedeckian ordered.

"I will do no such thing." Jade raised her chin, giving him a defiant look.

His hands moved to the controls for the shock collar locked around her neck. A shiver of dread crawled down her spine, but she refused to let him see her fear. Her plan to escape had not worked out in her favor. She had severely underestimated the ruthlessness of the Vedeckian commander.

Before the Vedeckian could administer the shock, the other alien grabbed his hand.

"You can't shock her, Kafri. Commander Kadica said that she will not fetch as many credits if she is unconscious."

"Who cares? I just want the bitch off the ship after what she did to Kragan."

Jade bit back an indignant protest. Commander Kadica

had been the one to kill Kragan. Admittedly, it was because she had been holding a gun to the crewmember's head at the time. She had foolishly thought that holding one of his crew captive would give her a bargaining chip. She had been wrong. The commander had shot Kragan himself, and the shock of his head exploding in her face stupefied her long enough for the commander to coolly take the gun away from her.

Once he had the weapon, he struck with an almost casual hand, but the blow had knocked her unconscious. When she awoke, she had been fitted with the shock collar. Although the commander kept his face impassive, she saw the sadistic delight in his eyes when he proceeded to demonstrate to her how it worked.

When she regained consciousness the second time, Kwaret had been placing cool cloths on her bruised cheek. She was no longer in the cell with the other women. Instead, she was in a small room, barely large enough for the cot she was lying on. Just as in the larger cell, three walls were composed of white metal while the fourth was glass.

"I wish you had not attempted to escape," Kwaret had said softly.

"Yeah, well, I'm glad I did. Did you expect me to just wait around and see what you bastards have in mind for me?"

"I suppose not." He tugged a little at the rigid metal band surrounding her neck and shook his head. "But I'm afraid this makes you more vulnerable to them."

"I won't give in to them," she said fiercely. "Never. I'll never stop looking for a way to escape."

"I don't suppose you would believe me if I told you that help is coming? And that you just need to trust me and be patient?"

"Trust you?" She snorted. "I don't believe in trust anymore, nor in patience. If you want something, you have to go after it yourself."

"I suspected that that would be your response." Kwaret smoothed a cream around the edge of the collar. It burned like hell, and she tried to jerk away, but then a soothing numbness spread out from the cream. "Can I just ask, for your own sake, that you try and avoid antagonizing them?"

"You keep saying *them*. Aren't these your people?"

"They stopped being my people the day they started selling sentient beings for profit." He looked at her, red eyes solemn. "I am trusting you by telling you that."

Even though she scowled at him, rather than responding, part of her was impressed by his honesty. Based on what she had seen so far on board the ship, even the suggestion that he might betray his crewmates would probably result in very unpleasant consequences.

Kwaret made no further attempt to convince her, but she did her best to follow his advice even though it went against all of her natural instincts. She had never been good at holding her tongue. But then again, not holding her tongue had been what started this whole terrible chain of events. The usual wave of guilt washed over her, but she pushed it away with a practiced familiarity.

The lights in the corridor had dimmed twice before Kwaret reappeared. She had seen enough of the Vedeckians by now to pick up on the subtle indications that he was worried.

"What is it?"

"We have docked on Driguera. They have decided to sell you."

Fighting back a flare of panic, she gave a sardonic laugh. "So much for that help you promised."

"I believe that it is on the way, but I can't guarantee that it will be here in time."

He lowered his voice even further as he bent over her, running a scanner over her collar.

"I am resetting the frequency in your collar. It will still shock you, but it should not render you unconscious." His forehead creased slightly, what she interpreted as a sign of deep concern for the generally impassive Vedeckian. "But if you are shocked, I suggest you let them believe that it was successful. That may give you an opportunity to escape. I hope it will not be necessary."

Despite his hopes, a short time later two crewmen had entered her cell, thrown a hooded cape over her head, and force-marched her to her current location. Now she was in a small, dirty room. A cot against one wall was piled with stained blankets, and the other side of the room held hanging racks covered with an assortment of clothing, all of which looked cheap, flashy, and skimpy.

"If you won't let me shock her, then you take her clothes off," Kafri muttered.

Despite her underlying horror, she had to bite back a satisfied smile. Her training might not have been enough to keep her from being captured, but it had instilled a healthy fear in her captors. She had found out the first time one of them laid hands on her that the Vedeckians had their genitalia in the same place as human men and they were apparently equally as sensitive.

Of course, that was before the shock collar.

They looked at each other and she tensed. Kafri feinted to the right and she turned with him, trying to keep an eye on the other male. But Kafri grabbed her hand and held her long enough for the second male to take hold of her hoodie and rip it off her body, leaving her in her tight-fitting jogging tank and yoga pants. They stepped back, surveying her.

"She is quite small," Kafri said derisively, running his eyes over her breasts.

Apparently, even aliens preferred big-breasted women. Good. That meant they would be less interested in her.

"Perhaps they would be more enticing if they were not bound so tightly?"

They started to move into position again, and even though she was prepared this time, she still heard the fabric of her tank rip, leaving her clad only in her sports bra. The chilly temperature in the room hardened her nipples as both aliens stared at them.

"Is that a sign of arousal?" Kafri asked.

"Perhaps she likes this," the other sneered. "Commander Kadica may have been right about the type of master for whom she is best suited."

"He said we should find someone who's looking for some spirit. She doesn't look like she put up a fight." Kafri pulled out a knife and her heart hammered against her chest. "But I can take care of that."

Five minutes later, all three of them were breathless, and she was glad to see all of them were bleeding. Unfortunately, it was a small consolation. Her jogging pants were in tatters, sliced almost to the waistband over one hip and revealing a long strip of golden skin and an equally long red scratch where the knife had caught her. Her sports bra was tattered too, the torn fabric hanging by a thread from her right shoulder and the left side gaping open to reveal most of one small breast. More scratches covered her shoulders and her breasts.

She supposed she should be grateful they were not trying to injure her—none of the cuts were deep, even though she could feel the sting of each shallow mark.

"That's better, Keroud. She'll appeal to those buyers who prefer the challenge of breaking a more spirited slave."

"No one is going to break me," she snarled.

Keroud shook his head. Was that a fleeting flash of sympathy in his red eyes? "Everyone can be broken."

"Do you think that works?" Kafri asked, inspecting her.

"If they're looking for a fighter, yes."

"The commander spread the word that's what he was selling." Kafri shrugged. "I just hope some rich bastard is willing to pay to take her off our hands. And speaking of hands... Hold them out, human."

When she just glared at him, he sighed, and the two of them moved into position again. A few painful—for all of them—minutes later, her hands were cuffed in front of her, and a leash extended from the cuffs to Kafri.

"You're going to come with us now, like a good little human. If you struggle, I will yank you off your feet and drag you. Do you understand?"

She nodded reluctantly. As much as it galled her to comply with any of their orders, being dragged along like a piece of meat wouldn't do anything to help the situation.

"Good." He grinned, showing very sharp teeth. "Perhaps you can be trained after all."

He tugged sharply on the leash, and she stumbled but managed to stay on her feet, thankful that at least they hadn't removed her shoes, as he marched out of the room. They proceeded down the hallway, ending up in an area that reminded her disconcertingly of the backstage area from her brief foray into high school musicals. There were other women present, from a variety of other species, most of them standing meekly beside their captors. The only exception was a catlike female who growled and tried to scratch the tentacled alien holding her leash, but the ends of her fingers were bleeding and her handler only laughed.

"That one might be some competition," Kafri said quietly. "She's the only other one with any spirit."

"I doubt it. They've already declawed her. Probably yanked her fangs as well. She won't last long."

Jade closed her eyes to mask her instinctive horror. *Will someone do that to me too?*

"Don't worry, human. Your pathetic little nails are just enough to excite, not damage."

Somehow, that didn't make her feel any better.

One by one, each of the other females disappeared through the curtain at the far end of the room. None of them returned. At last, it was down to her and the feline female. Her captor dragged the other female yowling through the curtain.

Kafri had been studying a tablet while Keroud kept his eye on her, and a few minutes later he looked up, flashing those shark-like teeth.

"You were right. She didn't fetch much." He leaned closer to her. "We still have a few big buyers out there. You'd better hope you sell for a lot of credits—you might live longer as a valuable purchase."

Rather than responding, she headbutted him, smiling when she heard his nose crack and saw purple fluid drip down his face.

He snarled and reached for the control to the shock collar, but once again, Keroud stopped him.

"Conscious, remember? Her new owner will teach her manners soon enough."

Kafri glared at her as his hand dropped away from the controls and he snatched her leash. Almost dragging her off her feet again, he marched across the room and through the curtain. On the other side of the curtain, two aliens waited. Easily over eight feet tall, they were painfully thin with grey skin and oversized bald heads. They looked so much like an Earth stereotype of an alien that she had the oddest impulse to giggle but fought it back, afraid that it would turn into sobs.

One of them took the leash from Kafri and she immediately yanked at it, hoping to take him by surprise. Unfortunately, those deceptively thin limbs were stronger than they looked. He simply lifted the leash over her head, pulling her arms up until she was suspended on tiptoes trying to relieve the strain.

"A fighter?" The grey alien nodded his approval. "We have had a special request for this type of slave."

"I'll make sure he regrets that request," she growled, but the alien only nodded.

"Excellent. You may await the results of the sale in a reception room," he added, turning to Kafri and Keroud.

"We wished to watch the auction, Master Eiran," Kafri protested.

"There is a live feed."

"We would prefer to be in the audience. I want to see who takes her."

The grey alien tittered. "Oh, no. We would never breach our clients' confidentiality that way. Please accompany my assistant, Honorable Sirs."

Turning his back on the Vedeckians, Master Eiran led her through another set of curtains, keeping her on tiptoes as she tried not to fall. He paused to consult with another of his species.

"That is not the usual attire for a slave," the other alien complained.

"Perhaps not, but considering her classification, I suspect it is most appropriate."

"I bow to your wisdom, Esteemed Master."

Her captor pulled her through yet another set of curtains into a small round room surrounded by draperies. A bright overhead light illuminated the area as he fastened her leash to an overhead pole and stepped back to regard her thoughtfully.

"Under normal circumstances, I would warn you not to fight, but in this situation you may do whatever you wish. If someone damages you, then they will have purchased you."

He disappeared through the curtain, and a moment later, the surface on which she was standing began to rise until she was no longer backstage. Her platform was now surrounded by eight arched windows. The overhead light was too bright for her to make out anything behind the glass but then the panes slid silently upwards. A cacophony of noise erupted, and she realized that each window led into a small viewing room. She couldn't see much of the interior of the rooms, but her nose was assaulted by a variety of unpleasant smells.

A slithering sound came from one of the rooms, and she saw a yellow light flash over the opening. A moment later, a snake-like alien slithered into view. His head reminded her of a cobra's and his body looped below him in long coils, but he had two small arms. One of them reached for her face. She whipped her head around and bit down hard on a two-fingered hand. Her mouth filled with acidic blood and she released her grip, spitting the blood to the ground. The alien hissed angrily and his tail coiled around her legs with bone-crushing pressure. A red light flashed overhead, and she heard the slave master's voice.

"May I remind you, Honorable Sir, that any damage you cause will result in a forfeit of your deposit?"

The alien hissed again and let her go, slithering back to his room.

"Would any other interested party care to inspect the merchandise?"

Another light flashed yellow, and a new alien stepped out onto her platform. He was humanoid—just. Heavily furred, with short legs and longer arms extending from broad shoulders, he bore a faint resemblance to a gorilla and was easily twice her size. He wore a metal vest studded with spikes, each tip painted red, with matching cuffs around his wrists. Unlike the first alien, he made no attempt to approach her at first, simply circling her and studying her from all sides.

When he finally decided to come closer, she grabbed hold of her leash, putting all of her weight on her cuffs, and twisted her body to kick out at him, catching him in his broad midsection. Her arms felt as if they were being pulled out of their sockets, and her feet ached as if she had slammed them against the concrete wall. He just laughed.

"This one definitely has some possibilities." He studied her face. "If you try that again, I'll make you regret it."

The smug assurance in his voice infuriated her and when he approached a second time, she repeated the maneuver, aiming lower this time. He gave an outraged howl as her feet connected with something much softer. *Another alien male with genitalia between his legs*, she thought triumphantly, but a minute later, his hands were around her throat above the collar.

"I see you want to make your life interesting." He squeezed tighter. "I believe in making the punishment fit the crime. I wonder how you would look spread-eagle on an iron bar with my cock jammed down your throat?"

She could hear Master Eiran protesting and black spots were flashing in her vision, but she gathered her last strength and spat at him. To her shock, he laughed and released her.

"I'll take her. How much?"

Before the grey alien could respond, an alarm sounded and red lights began flashing in every one of the surrounding rooms. Another of the gorilla-like aliens came rushing out and grabbed her tormentor's arm.

"Lord Gokan, it's the Patrol. We have to leave. Now."

The alien grunted and reached for her leash. Dread washed over her as she realized he was planning on taking her with them, but when his fingers touched the leash, there was a bright spark. She felt the jolts of electricity run through her body as he growled and stepped back, shaking his hand.

"Sir, we don't have time for this."

"Very well." He leaned closer and, to her disgust, jammed a thick purple tongue into her mouth. She tried to bite down but he dug his thumb into her jaw, keeping her jaws open for his assault. He drew back and laughed. "Don't forget me, human. I have every intention of finding you—and teaching you a lesson."

He and his companions disappeared through the viewing room as one of the grey aliens rushed out. Just as he reached for her leash, more lights came on. A new species of alien surrounded them.

"Hold it right there," one of them ordered, and her captor froze.

Jade's heart pounded as she looked around at the influx of strange aliens. They weren't quite as tall as the grey aliens, but they were strongly built with heavily muscled bodies. Various shades of patterned green skin covered almost reptilian features, and she could have sworn she saw a tail whipping behind one of them.

Had she just been thrown from the frying pan into the fire?

CHAPTER THREE

"Down, Dada," his daughter demanded.

Inzen did his best not to show his reluctance as he leaned over and carefully placed Lily on the ground. His tail flicked after her, equally reluctant to let her go. She was so small and helpless and, unfortunately, utterly fearless. He knew he was being overprotective, but he couldn't stand the thought of anything happening to the little girl who held his heart in her tiny hand.

"What a little adventurer," Abby said, laughing as Lily toddled off after Abby's two girls, her beloved stuffed toy dangling from one pudgy little hand.

They were sitting on the back porch of the cozy house that Hrebec, his former captain, had built for his human mate. Abby had been one of a small group of females they rescued from a Vedeckian slave ship. Lily had also been one of their captives, and Inzen had willingly assumed responsibility for her. But as she grew, he found himself constantly worried about her health and safety, and his concerns were the reason for his visit.

While he admired the rolling countryside, carpeted in the

bright greens and purples of Trevelor, he found the rural quiet disturbing. He missed the constant hustle and bustle that surrounded his house in Wiang, the capital city.

"That is the problem," he said, returning to the subject of his visit. "She is so fearless, but she is so delicate. I cannot stand the thought of anything happening to her."

Abby reached over and patted his hand. He allowed the touch, recognizing it as a friendly gesture, even though his instincts wanted him to pull away.

"All parents feel like that." Her eyes softened. "Didn't you feel like that with your first daughter?"

"I suppose I must have, but I was so young back then. I thought the future was assured."

How wrong he had been. First his mate and then his daughter had been taken from him by the horrible plague they called the Red Death. It had wiped out every Cire female on Ciresia and left him a shadow of the male he used to be.

The little girl currently pulling up handfuls of feather grass had changed everything.

"But now I know how quickly everything can change," he continued. "All of you humans are so fragile. I am concerned that she will come to harm because I do not know enough about your species."

"I don't know everything about Tiana," Abby pointed out, referring to her adopted Cire daughter who was the same age as Lily. "Don't you think I worry about her too?"

He knew she had a point, but Abby had Hrebec to assist her. He watched Tiana as she tottered over to Lily. Her steps were just as uncertain, but she had her little tail to help her balance. She plopped down next to Lily and started pulling up handfuls of feather grass as well. Lily tilted her head, studying the plant, then happily stuffed a handful in her mouth.

"She is eating the feather grass!" He raced over and pulled

Lily into his arms, frantically trying to scoop the half-chewed vegetation out of her mouth.

The sudden movement shocked her and she started to cry, big brown eyes filling with tears that ran down and joined with the purple drool from the grass. Her sobs tore him apart and he snuggled her against his chest, his tail patting soothingly at her tiny back as he murmured reassurances.

"Inzen, calm down. It's not poisonous and they all do it." Abby came up beside him and patted his arm reassuringly before she reached for Lily. "Come here, sweetheart. Let's get you cleaned up."

He would have refused, but Lily had already pushed herself towards Abby and he reluctantly let her go. Unable to let her out of his sight, he trailed behind as Abby carried the baby up on the porch and cleaned her face with swift efficiency. Lily was all smiles again as she lunged for him this time. She gave him a big hug, her little arms tightening around his neck, and once again wiggled to get down.

"Don't worry, Unca Inzen. I'll watch her," Lucie said. She was Abby's oldest daughter and liked to be in charge of everything, even though she was still a child herself.

He and Abby watched the children play for a little while—without any attempt to eat the vegetation this time—before he turned to her.

"What am I going to do? I worry about her so much, but I do not want her to be afraid."

"You're doing a fine job, Inzen. She's obviously loved and happy," Abby said firmly, but then she sighed. "But I agree that you can't put your fears on her. I've seen children crippled by their parents' fears."

She stared out across the fields, frowning thoughtfully. "How's Cassie doing? With Angel?"

Cassie was another of the human females they had rescued

and both she and her daughter, Angel, shared his house in town. Cassie operated a small but successful clothing business from the ground floor of the house.

"Very well," he said proudly. He thought of the girl as another daughter. "Her business is thriving. She keeps Angel in the shop with her as much as she can, and I help out when she lets me. You know how independent she is."

"Doesn't that help? To see how she interacts with her daughter?"

"To a certain extent, yes. But I think it is harder for me in some ways because I already know what it is like to lose a child."

"It probably also helps that she has her shop to focus on," Abby said softly. "She can't spend all her time worrying."

Was she suggesting that he find employment? He sponsored a training school and gave lessons there a few times a week, but he did not need the income and could think of nothing more important than raising a child. Before he could respond, Abby frowned again.

"Has Cassie shown any interest in a boyfriend?"

"A boy? As a friend? I do not understand. Why would she want to be friends with a young male?"

"No, I mean a male. A romantic interest."

He shook his head as he understood the direction of Abby's thoughts. He also worried about Cassie's obvious distrust for males of any species. Although she had told him enough about her past for him to know she had been abused by those she should have been able to trust, he hoped that someday she would be able to move past it.

"She says that she is not interested and I am not willing to push the matter."

"Maybe I should talk to her," Abby said thoughtfully.

"Please do not. Let her take the time she needs to come to terms with her past."

"What if she never does?"

"Then that will be her decision."

Abby's brows drew together, but to his relief, she nodded. He knew her intentions were good, but he had heard enough of Cassie's nightmares to know she was far from ready to handle the other woman's interference, no matter how well-meaning.

"Abigail!" Hrebec strode out onto the back porch. "I have just received the oddest message."

"Daddy!" Lucie grabbed Tiana and Lily's hands and came rushing over.

Lily climbed up onto Inzen's lap while Hrebec reached down and lifted his girls into his arms. His tail reached out to curve around Abby's wrist and she smiled up at her family.

"Girls, I need to talk to Mama for a minute." Hrebec placed the girls back on the ground. "If you go into the kitchen, I brought you all a little treat."

"Cookies?" Lucie asked.

"Why don't you go find out?" Abby laughed. "But only one each."

Once again, the three girls trotted off and Inzen did his best not to think about all the possible dangers that awaited them in the kitchen.

"You spoil them," Abby scolded Hrebec. He laughed and scooped her up, sitting back down with her on his lap.

"It is a father's right to spoil his girls. Is that not right, Inzen?"

"Oh, I know he'll be on your side." One of Abby's eyes fluttered shut in an odd gesture as she looked at him. "You're a big softie too, aren't you?"

"I am not soft." A Cire warrior was never soft.

"It's just an expression. It means you have a very kind

heart. Both of you," she added hastily when Hrebec growled. "Not that I'm not glad to see you, but why are you home so early? I thought you wanted to finish that table today."

Hrebec had taken up woodworking since he renounced his ship in order to spend more time with his wife and daughters.

"I received a message from Kwaret." Hrebec studied Inzen. "You remember that he infiltrated that Vedeckian ship in hopes of discovering if they planned to return to Earth again?"

Although the Vedeckians were an evil race, quite willing to sell illegal slaves if the profit margin was high enough, Kwaret was an exception. Inzen had to admit that the Vedeckian male had proven helpful on more than one occasion.

"Did they return to Earth?" he asked.

"I am afraid so. They kidnapped three females and two infants."

Abby gasped, her eyes going wide. "Oh, those poor women."

"Captain Armad also received a message from Kwaret and is on his way to intercept the ship. He should be able to reach them before they attempt to sell the females. In accordance with standard protocol, they intend to wipe their memories and return all of them to Earth, but there may be a problem."

"Don't tell me one of them fell in love with a Vedeckian," Abby gasped.

"No, that is not it." Hrebec looked over at Inzen, his eyes compassionate. "One of the females claims that her daughter was already stolen. A year ago. Her mate was killed at the time and she has been searching ever since."

Lily. His mind went blank as despair washed over him. He couldn't lose another daughter.

"No! Not my Lily." He rose to his feet and began pacing the length of the porch. "Perhaps she is looking for another child. Or perhaps she means Ginger."

Another unaccompanied infant, Ginger had been adopted by one of the other human females and her Cire mate. He was immediately ashamed of his selfish hope that this unknown female was searching for her instead and tried frantically to think of another possibility.

"What if this female is not telling the truth? How do you know she is not lying?"

"Inzen, why would she lie?" Sorrow shadowed Abby's face. "No one would get on board a spaceship unless they were desperate."

"Did she choose to come?" he demanded.

Hrebec shook his head. "Based on what I was told, she was kidnapped with the others."

"You see?" he said triumphantly.

"But why would she lie?" Abby repeated.

"Perhaps she does not want to go back to a primitive planet. I mean no offense, Abby, but Earth is quite backward compared to our civilization. Or perhaps she cannot go back. Perhaps she is some type of criminal." The possibilities raced through his mind, each one more horrible than the last.

"I do not believe you are being entirely rational," Hrebec said.

"Would you be rational if it was your daughter?"

"I suppose not," his captain admitted. "But we do not yet know that she is searching for Lily. We do not even know how many times the Vedeckians have been to Earth. Once we acquire the Vedeckian ship, we can examine their records, but you know that it will take time to break through their encryption."

"Where is this female now?"

"On the Vedeckian ship, heading for Driguera. That is why Kwaret contacted me. He was not sure that his message had reached Captain Armad, but even if it had, he knew the Patrol would order the *Defiance* to return the other females to Earth and it would be at least a month before he could bring the female here to Trevelor."

A month? A month where he would not know if he was going to lose his daughter. He shuddered at the thought. And if, Granthar forbid, this female did turn out to be Lily's mother, he could not keep her from her daughter. A sudden, foolish impulse possessed him.

"Driguera is only a few days from here," he said slowly. "What if I go and retrieve her?"

"You?" Hrebec stared at him and then turned to look at Abby, who was also regarding him with a thoughtful expression. "What do you think, Abigail?"

"Would you take Lily with you?" she asked.

His feelings warred with each other. He hated the idea of being separated from his daughter, even briefly, but there was no way he would expose her to this strange female until he was sure she was worthy. He took a deep breath, already hating the idea.

"I do not think it would be a good idea for her to accompany me. Would you care for her while I was gone?"

"Of course we will. But wouldn't you rather leave her with Cassie?"

"I do not want to ask her when she already has so many responsibilities with her shop and with Angel." He looked at her anxiously. "But perhaps it would be too much for you also?"

Abby laughed. "No, it's fine. My responsibilities these days are strictly confined to children. And my mate." She put a hand to Hrebec's cheek. "Do you mind?"

"No, my love. A house full of children is a house full of joy." He turned back to Inzen. "When will you leave?"

His heart ached, already regretting the separation, but a

warrior never avoided a painful duty. "Right now. That is, after I return to the city and pack some clothes and toys for her first."

"Don't worry about that." Abby waved a hand. "She and Tiana are about the same size and I have plenty of clothes."

"Very well. Here, you may need this." He handed Abby the small device.

"What is it?"

"A tracking device."

"You put a chip in her?" Her eyes went wide with shock.

"What? No, of course not. It is for her Bobo." He looked out to where the girls had been playing and saw the toy abandoned on the ground. Purple drool covered one ear and he sighed as he retrieved it and handed it to Abby. "It is her favorite, but she has an unfortunate tendency to lose it."

He had put a transmitter in the toy after one long, painful night when he hadn't been able to find it and she'd cried for hours.

"That's brilliant." Abby reached for Bobo, then frowned. "Is this the same toy she had on the ship?"

"Yes. Is it some type of Earth animal?"

"A fox, I think, although it's so worn it's hard to know for sure." She smiled up at him. "I'll be sure to keep track of it while you're gone."

Saying goodbye to Lily made his chest ache, but she was happily absorbed in eating her cookie with her new friends and, other than giving him a big sloppy kiss, didn't seem to even notice his departure. As he strode away, he prayed to Granthar with all his might that the strange female was not Lily's mother.

CHAPTER FOUR

Jade stared up at the large green aliens surrounding her on the sale platform and did her best to look fierce, even though her heart thudded against her ribs.

"Do not be afraid, female. I am Ensign Zastav of the Confederated Planets Patrol ship, *Defiance*. We are here to free you and return you to your planet."

Despite the grandiose words, the male addressing her sounded somewhat uncertain and she relaxed a little. She relaxed even more when he hissed at the collar around her neck and demanded that Master Eiran hand over the key. He unlocked it and threw it to the ground in disgust.

"Do not worry, female. All of those involved in this barbaric activity will be punished."

"I'm happy to hear that, but please, call me Jade."

"As you wish... Jade."

When the skin over his cheeks darkened, she suspected that, despite his size and forbidding appearance, he was quite young.

Zastav and his team escorted her back to the ship, a

phalanx of the big warriors surrounding her as they marched through the streets of what appeared to be some type of trading port. They had handed her a cloak but, unlike the Vedeckians, did not insist on keeping her hooded and she caught brief glimpses of the town between their bodies. It reminded her of some of the markets she had encountered on her buying trips. Small crowded stalls, a dizzying array of colors, and a wide variety of items for sale—many of which she didn't recognize. Strange scents wafted through the air, and she saw an astonishing variety of aliens during those brief glimpses. If it hadn't been for her driving need to find her daughter, she would have loved to explore the port.

Rather than returning her to the Vedeckian ship, Zastav took her to his ship and escorted her to his captain. Captain Armad was a large alien with shaggy fur and a rather disturbing resemblance to a bear but he was extremely polite and deferential. He apologized profusely for their kidnapping and informed her that they would be returned to Earth at once, adding with another apology that their memories of the experience would be erased.

"You can't do that," she protested immediately.

"I'm afraid it is a requirement. Your planet is not yet ready for the knowledge of more advanced civilizations."

She glared at him. "If you were truly an advanced civilization, you wouldn't let people be kidnapped and sold into slavery."

"I understand your point, but all civilizations have those who break the law. We still cannot permit our existence to be discovered. Besides, would anyone on your planet believe you if you tried to tell them what happened?"

"Probably not. But in my case, it doesn't matter. I'm not returning."

He frowned at her, his ear flicking forward, and she tried

not to flinch at the intimidating display. "What do you mean not returning? You belong on your planet."

"No, I don't. My daughter is out here somewhere and I'm going to find her."

"Your daughter?"

It was hard to tell through the fur, but he looked shocked.

"Kwaret didn't tell you? My daughter was taken a year ago by another Vedeckian ship."

He shook his head. "No, I haven't spoken with him yet. He is still locked up with the other Vedeckians."

"You locked him up? Isn't he the one who led you here? You need to let him go right now," she demanded.

"Don't worry. We will. But it was necessary to maintain the illusion that he is simply another crew member so that he can continue his work."

"Continue? You mean you think they'll try again?"

"We hope not. But the ship that seized you was on its second visit."

For the first time, she wondered how many others had been kidnapped along with her daughter. She thought she remembered a rumor about another woman and child going missing, but she had been too consumed by her own search to pay much attention.

"You said 'second' visit. Who was taken the first time? It wasn't just my daughter, was it?"

The captain sighed, and his ears drooped.

"No, I'm afraid not. We know a female and her son were taken by this ship. We are going through the records now to find out if there were others. We do know that another ship we intercepted last year had two unaccompanied infants on board."

"You found two babies last year?" Her heart started to pound. "Did you return them to Earth?"

"Who would we have returned them to? The records were not sufficiently detailed for us to be able to track down the location and we cannot appear on your world."

"So you might have my daughter?"

Excitement coursed through her veins.

"It is possible, but I make no guarantees. Remember that the two were found on another ship."

Unable to remain seated, she started pacing the room. "I want to see them. Where are they?"

"On a planet called Trevelor." The captain clicked his claws thoughtfully on his desk. "Once we return the other females to Earth, we could take you there—*if* you do not wish to remain on Earth."

"Of course I don't want to stay on Earth without my daughter. How long will the trip take?"

"Approximately three of your weeks, perhaps four."

She stared at him in dismay. Another month? When she was so close after such a long time?

"Is there another alternative? Can I hire a ship—"

She stopped abruptly as she realized she had nothing with which to make purchases. All of her wealth was back on Earth and did nothing for her now. The only thing she had of value was the slim gold Rolex around her wrist, and she doubted that aliens would be impressed by the Earth brand. Still, perhaps it would be worth something. She also had the jade ring her grandmother gave her on her twenty-first birthday. Although she hated to part with it, material goods mattered little in comparison to her daughter.

"That may not be necessary," the captain said slowly. "Kwaret also communicated with the Cire settlement on Trevelor. I believe they are sending someone to take you there."

"I don't understand. If that's true, why did you say you would return me to Earth?"

"It was a test," he said. "To see which you valued more: your child or your planet."

"You mean I have to choose? If I go after my daughter, does that mean I can never return to Earth?"

"That is the official position of the Patrol. Contact is always risky and must be limited."

Jade stared at him. Of course she would not return home without her daughter, but once she found her, what would become of them? She thought about the grandmother for whom her daughter was named. The original Hana had come to the United States on her own, unable to speak a word of English. She had turned a small mending operation into an international clothing business by the time she retired in her 80s. If her grandmother could do it, so could she.

"Then I'll stay."

"You have no kin?"

Why did she feel the sudden urge to cry? Her parents died in a car crash when she was in her teens, but she had never been close to them, spending most of her time with her grandmother instead. She had loved her sobo fiercely, but she had died the year before her daughter was born. All of the people she had thought were friends had drifted away over the past year, unable to deal with her sorrow—or her relentless search for her daughter.

"No." She shook her head. "No one is going to miss me."

Except perhaps the stockholders. She suspected that her Board of Directors would run the business into the ground within a few years, but that no longer mattered. Hana was all that mattered.

"Very well." Captain Armad nodded. "I will inform you once the emissary arrives. In the meantime, do you wish to rejoin your companions?"

"Yes, please."

Ashley and Naomi were in the medical bay surrounded by more of the big green aliens who she learned were a race called the Cire. They treated all of the women with the utmost respect and were fascinated and awed by the babies. Jade let one of the deferential males bandage her wounds, shaking his head the entire time, and accepted a medical gown to cover up her torn clothing.

Then she settled in to wait, hoping desperately that she was close to finding her daughter at last.

CHAPTER FIVE

By the time Inzen arrived at Driguera, his nerves were completely frayed. He had spent the trip missing Lily with every breath he took and alternating between fear and anger that this unknown human female might prove to be her biological mother.

She can't be much of a mother, he tried to tell himself. After all, she had not even been with her daughter when she disappeared. But no matter how hard he tried to convince himself, he knew there were all too many reasons why they might have been separated.

As soon as he touched down, he headed for the *Defiance*. This had been his ship once, and he had enjoyed his years serving under Hrebec, but he was too anxious to feel any nostalgia as he entered the ship.

"Chief Engineer Inzen." A young Cire crewman greeted him with a formal salute. "I am Ensign Zastav."

"It is simply Inzen now. Where are the—" He stopped himself from demanding to be escorted to the human females. There was protocol to be observed. "Where is your captain?"

"He is waiting for you outside the medical bay."

"Medical bay?" He turned immediately and strode in that direction, the young male hurrying to catch up with him.

"Is there something wrong?" he demanded. "Have the human females been injured? Or the infants?"

"No, sir. Well, not most of them."

"What do you mean?"

"One of the females has some injuries. It seems she chose to fight the Vedeckians."

The young male sounded both shocked and approving. Cire females did not fight, but their society valued courage. Inzen grinned fiercely, impressed despite himself.

"Good. A mother should always protect her child."

"But this is the one without a child," Zastav said breathlessly.

Inzen almost stumbled. His tail flicked to one side, balancing him, as he resumed his swift pace. Was this fierce female Lily's mother?

"And should not a female protect herself as well?" he asked.

"But that is why Granthar made us warriors—to protect our females."

"It does not appear that these females had any warriors to protect them," he said dryly.

"I would protect them. To my death."

Inzen had no doubt that the boy's words were genuine and he nodded his approval. "Then you are a worthy male."

Up ahead, he saw Captain Armad waiting for them. A large, furry male, he was an Afbera rather than a Cire warrior, but he had proven to be an honorable and reliable captain.

"Thank you for coming, Chief Engineer Inzen. Kwaret informed us that he sent a message to Captain Hrebec." He lowered his voice. "You understand that the female may be the parent of one of the infants rescued last year?"

"I understand," he said grimly.

"We had intended to return all of them to their planet after wiping their memories, but she is insisting that she wishes to remain to look for her daughter."

"I am here to take her to Trevelor. To see if perhaps..." The words caught in his throat.

Captain Armad looked relieved. "I think that is the best solution. We have been ordered to return the other females as quickly as possible. Do you wish to meet her now?"

No.

"I suppose I must."

The captain slid aside the panel to the medical bay. Three human females were spread throughout the room. A tall one with red hair leaned against the front wall, talking to an obviously enamored Cire warrior, his tail constantly flicking in her direction. A small blonde one was seated on one of the tables sobbing, while two more males hovered over her. She had an infant cradled in her arms.

The third female was against the back wall, eyeing everyone suspiciously. She too was small, and holding an infant in her arms, but her hair was as dark and shiny as the wing of a kurosun. She looked up when he entered, and their eyes met across the room. He almost swayed at the impact. Her eyes were of the palest green, like the most secret parts of a female's body. His cock, which had barely bothered to stir in many years, suddenly stiffened.

What the hell was wrong with him? Why was he reacting to a human female, let alone one who would be returning to her planet in the very near future?

He forced his attention away from her and turned to the red-haired human. He could find no resemblance to his sweet daughter in this female, and the fear that had been haunting him since he began this journey loosened its grip.

"Captain Armad. Is this the emissary you promised me?" The pleasant, low-pitched voice interrupted his thoughts and he did not need to turn around to know that the dark-haired woman had approached. A hint of sweet, spicy fragrance reached his scent receptacles and his cock stiffened even further.

"And why is his tail touching me?"

He turned and found his tail had wrapped itself around the female's wrist. She looked surprised rather than angry as he hastily pulled it away, tilting her head to study him. Fuck. This was not the time to be distracted by a female, no matter how tempting. He forced himself to give a formal bow.

"I am Inzen Var'Narian."

"I'm Jade Arlington. Are you going to help me search for my daughter?"

His heart beat rapidly, and he couldn't tell if it was from relief or trepidation. *She* was the female? He looked closer and realized that she was dressed in a medical gown that swamped her small figure. A bandage disappeared under one sleeve, and he remembered the ensign's words. Someone had harmed this delicate female? His tail lashed angrily and he saw her eyes follow the movement.

"Is that not your child?" he asked, looking at the infant she carried.

"Justin? No, he belongs to Naomi." Her odd little mouth twisted in an endearing gesture. "I'm just holding him while she works her wiles on the crew."

"Wiles?"

"You know, flirts?"

He recognized the term from something Cassie had said, and he frowned.

"Cire warriors do not understand this flirting. They think she is looking for a mate."

Her brows drew together. "She already has one of those. Naomi," she called to the other female. "He thinks you're looking for a husband."

"Who says I'm not?" the female said.

"I think Stefan might object."

"But he isn't here, is he?"

Inzen drew in a shocked breath, but Naomi patted the warrior's tail and then came to join them. Behind her back, he could see the hopeless longing in the face of the young warrior. All of the systems that comprised the Confederated Planets had suffered from the plague known as the Red Death, but the Cire had suffered most of all. Their entire female population had died—or so they thought. But even with the discovery of a few isolated survivors, the prospect of a mate and children was out of reach for most Cire warriors. It was cruel for this female to toy with him.

"You should not have done that," he said sternly.

"Jeez, relax. I was only playing with him."

"I don't think he understands that, Naomi." Jade was also looking at the young male, her eyes sympathetic.

While he appreciated her concern, he did not like her looking at another male. He shifted his position so that he was between the two of them.

"You will come with me now," he ordered.

"Excuse me? I thought we weren't on a slave ship anymore."

He closed his eyes. Fuck, he was handling this badly.

"I apologize if I seemed peremptory. I understood that you wished to accompany me."

"You have news of my daughter?" she asked eagerly.

"Perhaps," he said evasively, unwilling to commit. "We

know that the Vedeckians made previous trips to your planet. We rescued one of those ships, and the females and infants we freed currently reside on the planet Trevelor."

An adorable scowl twisted her small features. "Why didn't you return them to Earth where they belonged?"

"None of the females chose to return."

Naomi's eyes widened. "You mean we don't have to go back?"

"Naomi, you can't want to stay here!" Jade exclaimed, and his heart sank.

If she did prove to be Lily's mother, she would also want to return. She would want to take his daughter away from him. He scanned her features, looking for a resemblance, but the astonishing variety of human features was still a mystery to him. Her hair was much darker than Lily's. Lily also didn't possess those stunning green eyes—his daughter's eyes were a soft brown.

As he studied Jade's face, he found himself admiring her delicate little features—so different from his own and yet so attractive. Her eyebrows were smooth arches above those amazing eyes, her funny little nose not as prominent as the other human females, and her mouth... He could easily envision tasting those full pink lips the way Hrebec tasted Abby's.

"Your tail is back," she said dryly, and he snatched it away from her wrist.

"I apologize."

"It's all right." She gave it a casual pat and his knees almost buckled. "I'm just still adjusting to all of this."

"Do you wish to remain on the ship with your companions?" he asked, unsure of which answer he wanted most.

She looked around the room, then shook her head, straightening her small shoulders.

"No. If there's any chance that one of those children is my Hana, then I want to go with you."

Equal portions of exhilaration and fear filled him, but he managed to keep his face and voice composed as he extended a hand to her.

"Then let us leave."

CHAPTER SIX

Jade stared up at the big Cire warrior offering her his hand. She had been standing in the medical bay, cradling Naomi's son and observing the other women, when he appeared. Surprisingly, neither of them seemed in a hurry to return to Earth. Ashley bloomed under the obvious interest of the Cire warriors, fluttering helpless eyelashes at them. Naomi's flirting was a lot less subtle. Jade tried her best to wait patiently but her nerves were beginning to fray by the time the door opened and a strange Cire appeared.

He looked around the room before their eyes met, but as soon as they did, she felt an odd little shock travel down her spine. *Is this the emissary?* She frowned as he turned back to Naomi, annoyed that he had dismissed her so quickly. Determined to get an answer, she went to join him.

When his tail curled around her wrist, she felt the same shock, like a jolt of recognition, but that was impossible. And then he turned to face her, big black eyes focusing on her face. Like the other Cires, he had a flat nose and a thin, almost lipless mouth, but the ridges running back over his skull were more pronounced, along with the small nubs that patterned his deep green skin. Even in a room full of big warriors, he stood out. But it was more than the impressive muscles revealed by his tight-fitting tunic. He had an air of authority that dominated the small room, and she suspected that he was older than the young males that made up the rest of the crew.

She drew in a quick breath and his spicy scent washed over her, comforting and exciting at the same time. When he confirmed that he was the one sent to accompany her to Trevelor, an unexpected sense of relief swept over her. To her own astonishment, she took his hand.

Jade followed the big Cire warrior through several corridors to the landing ramp, nerves tying her stomach in knots. Leaving Ashley and Naomi had been harder than she expected. Ashley cried when she left, and even Naomi cracked enough to give her a quick hug and wish her well. Now she was completely on her own in this strange new world. So far, the Cire had treated her with nothing but courtesy, but she didn't easily place her trust in the unknown. Yet something about this particular male made her feel oddly safe.

She rejected the notion as soon as it surfaced—the only person she could rely on was herself.

He paused at the top of the landing ramp, and she took the opportunity to look around. The sight that met her eyes was both like and unlike every science fiction movie she had ever seen. An astonishing array of spaceships met her eyes in a multitude of shapes and colors, but no movie could have captured the other aspects—the hum of machinery, the clanking and swearing from workers loading odd-looking cargo, and once again the astonishing variety of smells that wafted past her nose. She took a deep breath and realized that the predominant scent was that of the male next to her, a warm, spicy scent that made her want to rub her face against him. The thought made her nipples tighten and a pleasant ache start low in her belly.

Fuck! What was she thinking? This was no time for her long-neglected libido to make itself known.

He turned to look at her as if he could detect her arousal, but she kept her face calm. She had spent too many years in business meetings to let her emotions show. He studied her, his eyes drifting down over her body. If it had been anyone else, she would have been insulted, but the heat of his gaze felt almost like a caress and her arousal intensified.

Unable to help herself, her eyes flicked down below his belt, and it took all her self-control not to reveal her astonishment. The tight-fitting pants did little to conceal what she assumed was a massive erection—if that was his unaroused state, she couldn't imagine what he would be like fully hard. As it was, his size should have discouraged her from even thinking about the possibility of having... She hastily reeled in her thoughts. He was an alien, and no matter how nice he had been so far or how helpful he was being now, or how long it had been, she only had one purpose.

"Do you not have any other clothing?" he asked, interrupting her wayward thoughts.

"No, I don't. The Vedeckians didn't kidnap me with a suitcase," she snapped, pulling her cloak closed over her pitiful outfit.

The medic had provided her with what she assumed was a medical gown to cover up her torn clothes, but she was well aware that the garment was both ill-fitting and unflattering. Her fingers itched for a needle and thread. If nothing else, she would be able to make some repairs to her own clothing.

"I apologize," he said stiffly. "I meant no insult."

His tail withdrew, leaving her skin feeling unexpectedly

cool, and she suddenly realized that it had been encircling her wrist since they first stopped.

"I know you didn't." She reached out to give his tail a comforting pat, and he froze. "Did I do something wrong?"

"Not at all. That is a... friendly gesture amongst my people."

Ah. It must be similar to a handshake. She patted his tail again and smiled up at him.

"I hope we can be friends."

"Friends? Umm, yes. Friends would be... nice."

He seemed oddly discomforted and she wondered if she had overstepped. "I mean, if that's all right with you. I assumed your people were okay with humans."

He closed his eyes briefly. "Yes, we find humans very acceptable."

All righty then. She took another deep breath and ignored the wave of arousal that swept over her as she pulled more of his scent into her lungs.

"Shall we go to your ship?"

"I thought perhaps a short detour first."

"Why?" she asked suspiciously.

"I wish to pick up a few items to make your trip more pleasant."

He looked so hopeful that she ignored the alarm bells ringing in her head. This place's version of the police had entrusted her to him. Not that she had much faith in the police after what happened to Nathan and Hana, but surely that meant he was one of the good guys.

"It won't take long, will it?"

"Not at all."

Once again, he offered her his hand and this time, she didn't hesitate to place her hand on his. As they descended the ramp, his tail came up to curl around her waist but she decided to ignore it.

"Hold your hood over your head and keep your cloak closed," he ordered as they started across the landing field. "It is for your safety," he added when she glared at him. "Females are highly desirable, especially one like you."

Somewhat mollified, she obeyed as they reached the first of one of the many shopping streets that led away from the spaceport.

"What do you mean? One like me?"

"Soft, beautiful, fertile."

The final word made her heart ache. If only she had been—it would have saved so much time and so much money. She didn't care about the money, but she regretted all those years without her daughter.

"I don't think I'm any of those things," she snapped.

He started to respond but then the first shopkeeper—a tall grey alien who was obviously the same species as the slave auctioneer—hailed them. Her pulse started to race and she stopped dead in her tracks, but Inzen's tail tucked her gently up beside him as he opened negotiations. To her relief, he simply began bargaining for clothing. For her.

It was immediately clear that almost nothing would fit her without extensive alterations. Inzen frowned at the latest offering—a bronze silk affair that was almost as wide as it was tall—and started to shake his head.

"Do they have sewing equipment?" she asked softly. "Needles and thread? I can alter it to fit me."

"You are a seamstress?"

Among other things.

"Yes. I'm surprised you know that word."

"I live with one."

Before she could react, he turned back to the alien. The

male had been watching them intently, his eyes cutting to her every time she spoke, but he smiled ingratiatingly and started selecting sewing equipment from the shelves.

Why did the knowledge that Inzen lived with a female disturb her so? Despite what she was fairly sure was a mutual attraction, she didn't have time for complications. Pushing the curious disappointment out of her mind, she inspected the proffered supplies and made her selections. Inzen added several additional garments to the pile despite her protests before he completed the deal.

After the shopkeeper tied their purchases into a complicated arrangement of fabric, they turned to leave. A small alien suddenly darted up to them, crashing into Jade. It wasn't the first time someone had attempted to pickpocket her in a crowded market, and she reacted on instinct, her foot sweeping out as she grasped his arm—one of four—and whirled him around, yanking one of his arms up behind his back. Inzen reacted just as quickly, his hand at the alien's throat. He gave her an astonished look before he focused on the pickpocket.

"You dare to try and steal from my female?"

"N-no," the small figure stuttered.

A voluminous robe of many colors covered his slender form, and even though his features were unfamiliar, she suspected he was no more than a child.

"I will report you to the market master," Inzen said sternly.

"No, please, Honored Sir. Not that."

"What will they do to him?" she asked quietly.

"For stealing?" The alien in the stall behind them leaned forward, his face alive with interest. "He will lose at least one of his hands."

Inzen looked at her and then shook his head. "I cannot be responsible for that."

"Me either. Let him go." She dropped the arm she had been holding.

"I will as soon as he returns your ring."

With muttered apologies, the youngster reached into his robe and pulled out her jade ring. Despite her experience, she hadn't even realized he slipped it off her finger.

"It matches your eyes," Inzen said as he handed it back to her.

"I know—I have my father's eyes. And that's why my mother named me after the stone." She smiled up at him. "Thank you, Inzen. My grandmother gave me this ring and it means a lot to me."

"You are most welcome." He turned and scowled at the boy, an imposing sight. "Now go and stay out of trouble."

"Yes, Honorable Sir." The youngster nodded enthusiastically, muttering thanks and apologies as Inzen released him. He started to disappear into the crowd but turned back with an unexpectedly impish grin. "For at least the rest of the day."

Then he was gone. Jade burst out laughing, and Inzen ruefully shook his head. The stall keeper sighed.

"You know he'll be back at it within the hour."

"Perhaps. But he will still have all four hands."

"I'm not sure that will be much comfort to his victims," the alien muttered, but Jade smiled up at Inzen and tucked her hand in his arm.

"You did the right thing."

Did the skin across his cheekbones darken? Before she could decide, his tail was once more around her waist as he led them back across the landing field.

She looked up to find him studying her.

"What is it?"

"Your eyes," he said slowly. "Do all human children inherit their father's eye color?"

"Not at all. They could inherit from their mother or another relative. It depends on their genes. You understand genetics, right?"

"Of course. But all Cire have black eyes."

Now that he mentioned it, she realized that it was true, but despite the similarity in color, they were by no means identical. She already suspected that she would be able to recognize his eyes. "Why do you ask?"

"I wondered if your daughter would have green eyes."

"No." A lump appeared in her throat as she remembered Hana's sweet face.

She pushed her thoughts aside as Inzen headed for a tall, sleek ship. It resembled the aerospace version of a yacht, and she nodded approvingly. It looked fast and expensive.

Unfortunately, he didn't stop there. He led the way around the ship, and she saw another vessel. Small and squat, it had a neat paint job that did little to disguise the numerous dents that peppered the hull.

"Is that your ship?" She scanned the rest of the area hopefully. The only other ships in sight were larger cargo vessels.

"Yes. The *Flower* is my personal vessel." He smiled with obvious affection at what she probably would have called an old clunker.

"Is it, uh, fast?" She also wanted to ask if it was spaceworthy, but she suspected he would be insulted.

"Fast? It made the Kessel journey in under twelve parsecs."

"Is that good?" she asked doubtfully.

"No other ship in the squadron could match it." He looked down at her, his expression surprisingly sad. "Do not worry, letari. We will be on Trevelor soon enough."

INZEN WRESTLED WITH HIS CONSCIENCE AS HE ESCORTED

Jade on board the *Flower*. Should he tell her that his daughter was one of the two unaccompanied infants she was coming to meet? No, he decided again. There was no guarantee that Lily belonged to Jade, and he did not want to cause either of them additional strain while they were in close quarters. Very close quarters, he realized as he reluctantly removed his tail from around her waist.

The *Flower* was designed for fast, short trips with no more than one or two passengers. A narrow cockpit at the front of the ship contained two chairs and the instrument panel. Behind it was a small multipurpose open area. A seating area that could be converted into two bunks flanked one wall, while the other wall contained minimal cooking facilities and a small sanitary unit. Other than a small cargo area beneath the floor, the engines made up the rest of the ship.

Her sweet, spicy scent had already begun to permeate the small ship, and he realized with a grimace that he was destined to spend the entire trip with a constant erection. Ever since she had caressed his tail, he had been fighting the urge to pull her closer, and when she willingly placed her hand on his arm, showing her trust in him, his heart had skipped a beat.

Jade looked around, then nodded. "It looks much better in here than it does on the outside—I mean, it's fine on the outside. It's just a little, umm..."

"Do not worry, my letari. I am aware that the *Flower* is not the most beautiful of ships. But she is fast and true."

"What does that mean? Letari?"

"It means little warrior. I am ashamed that I let the young thief get so close to you, but I was impressed by your defensive skills."

"I've been training since my daughter was taken. I wanted to be able to defend her once I had her back."

"You should never have to defend yourself or your child."

"That hasn't been my experience."

"I am truly sorry. I wish that I could return and teach everyone who hurt you a lesson."

Her face softened, and she reached out and patted his tail again. Each touch of her hand went straight to his aching cock. Should he tell her that he had understated the matter when he said it was a friendly gesture? No, he decided. Despite his frustration, he didn't want to miss an opportunity to have her hands on him.

By Granthar! What was he thinking? She would only be with him for a short time, and when she found her daughter—hopefully *not* Lily—she would no longer be a part of his life. He cleared his throat.

"If you will strap yourself into the other seat, I will prepare for takeoff."

CHAPTER SEVEN

As soon as Jade sat in the copilot's chair, Inzen showed her how to fasten the harness, resisting the temptation to perform the task himself. Her small frame was swamped by the large chair and he frowned down at her.

"I need to check the harness to make sure it is secure. It is designed for a larger being."

After studying him for a moment, she nodded.

"All right."

Although she tried to hide it with a brave face, he could tell that she was nervous. He knelt down next to the chair so that he wouldn't loom over her. He ran his fingers lightly down the shoulder straps. Although he tried to avoid touching her, he could feel the warmth of her skin as he tested the fit. He moved to the leg straps that circled her thighs and snapped into the buckle over her stomach. He heard her breath catch and, a second later, caught the sweet scent of her arousal.

Concentrate on the task at hand, he ordered himself, but his hand almost trembled as he glided it over the junction between her legs. His hands never trembled.

"It needs to be tighter." His voice sounded strained even to his own ears.

"All right," she repeated, but this time she sounded breathless.

"I need to place my finger beneath the strap to make sure it is not too tight."

"Go ahead."

He slid a finger beneath the strap across her stomach and had to bite back a groan as he felt the heat of her skin through the thin medical gown. He wanted nothing more than to rip open the flimsy fabric and touch her. Instead, he forced himself to concentrate on adjusting the settings on the harness until the strap tightened, forcing more of his hand against her skin. He knew he should withdraw but lingered a moment longer, unable to resist looking at her.

Now that he was kneeling, his head was only slightly above hers and he could see directly into those amazing eyes. Her pupils had dilated, leaving only a ring of pale green, and those full lips were parted, her breath escaping in a soft pant. Small white teeth clamped down on a plump lower lip, and he wanted—more than he had wanted anything in a very long time —to explore that tempting little mouth. The air between them thickened, but he forced himself to his feet and in doing so, placed his cock directly in front of her face. He saw her tongue flick out to moisten those full lips, and his cock jerked as he imagined her taking him between them. The action was strictly forbidden. No Cire could afford to waste his seed in a female's mouth, but the image could not be erased. With more haste than dignity, he shoved himself out of the cockpit.

"I am going to perform a flight check and then we will depart."

She murmured something but he didn't dare look back at her.

Concentrating on his tasks did very little for his aching erection, but he forced himself to ignore it. He had only ever felt like this once before—when he met his mate—but even then, he didn't recall anything approaching the intensity of his need for her.

Mate?

The thought stopped him dead in his tracks. It was impossible. Their traditions dictated that a Cire form a mate bond only once. And yet, as he resumed his duties, he couldn't help but think of Hrebec and Abby. Admittedly, Hrebec had not been mated before but he had formed a mate bond with a human. Was it possible that even though he had been mated once, he could form a different but no less meaningful bond with Jade?

Pushing the thought aside to examine later, he returned to the pilot's chair and started the liftoff sequence. Jade leaned forward eagerly.

"This is very exciting. I couldn't see what it looked like when we left Earth."

Earth. Of course she would want to return to her planet. Even if his mating instinct had been aroused, he could not succumb to it. He would only be asking for heartache.

You are a warrior, he reminded himself. *You have the strength to resist the allure of this female.*

Despite his stern reminder, he did not feel as confident as he would like.

Jade watched eagerly as their small ship rose into the air. Inzen was apparently communicating with the planetary version of air traffic control because he hovered there for a moment before he received the signal to proceed. As soon as it came through, he took off, the planet falling away behind them with astonishing speed. She expected to find herself pushed back against the seat as they accelerated, but all she felt was a slight pressure against her chest. But even that minimal impact reminded her that her nipples were hard little buds. They had been pushing against the torn remnants of her sports bra since he had knelt beside her. And when he ran his hands down the straps, even though he had been nothing but respectful, she felt a rush of damp heat between her legs. And that finger against her skin, his big hand almost covering her entire stomach, had only heightened her arousal.

When he stood up, it was obvious that the arousal wasn't one-sided. A distant part of her brain reminded her that she was alone in a spaceship with an alien twice her size sporting a massive erection, but she felt no fear. Despite her tendency to assume that everyone had an ulterior motive, even in the brief time they had been together, something about Inzen had lowered her usual barriers.

Don't be ridiculous, she scolded herself. *You don't know him.* Just because he had been thoughtful enough to purchase clothes for her didn't mean she could trust him.

The ship burst out of the atmosphere into a dark sky. All she could see before her were stars, clear and bright and larger than she could have imagined. She automatically looked back over her shoulder but of course there was only the cabin behind them.

"Do you wish to see the planet?" Inzen asked that before she could agree, he had already turned the ship back around so that she could see the vast globe falling away behind them. Unlike Earth, the surface was etched in dark reds and browns, but it was an awe-inspiring sight.

"I never thought I would see anything like this," she said softly.

He sighed, his gaze also focused on the planet. "Neither did I."

"I don't understand. Aren't you a spaceship pilot?"

"I am now but I spent the majority of my life on my home planet. When the Red Death came, Ciresia became nothing more than a shell. I only left because there was nothing there for me anymore."

"The Red Death?"

"Kwaret did not explain?"

"We didn't exactly have a lot of time to talk."

"The systems in this sector belong to an organization called the Confederated Planets. More than twenty years ago, a plague swept across our civilization. It spared no one, but the Cire were in some ways the most devastated. We thought all of our females were lost to us."

"I'm so sorry. Did you lose someone you cared about?"

"My mate died in the first year. She had never been strong. But my daughter..." His hands clenched the controls, and she saw the skin of his knuckles turn almost white. "She stayed well for a long time, long enough that we thought perhaps she would survive. She did not."

His tail fluttered towards her and she put her hand on it, stroking it soothingly. He hissed, looking over at her with startled eyes.

"I know the words don't mean much, but I am truly sorry. It's been hard enough knowing that my daughter is missing. I can't imagine what it would be like to know that she was gone forever."

His tail wrapped around her hand now, and she wondered which one of them was soothing the other. They sat in silence for a few minutes before he spun the ship back around and headed out into the darkness of space. Then she remembered his earlier words.

"Did you find a new mate?"

"What?!" He looked as startled as if she had thrown a

bucket of water in his face. Maybe it was a taboo subject, but she really wanted to know.

"Back when we were shopping, you said you lived with a seamstress."

"Ah, yes." He sagged back down in his chair. "She is a young human female."

Why did that surprise her? Even aliens liked trophy wives.

"And she is your new mate?" She suspected that her tone was not as neutral as she would have liked.

"No, not at all. She is like a daughter to me." He hesitated, and his tail tightened around her hand. "I also have a much younger daughter."

"I see." He might not have mated again, but apparently, he hadn't hesitated to spread his seed around. S*top that*, she scolded herself. If his race was dying, it undoubtedly increased the importance of having children. He was an attractive, thoughtful male—he shouldn't have to be alone. But she found she had no interest in pursuing the subject of his daughter's mother or any of his other relationships. She changed the subject.

"How long will it take to get to Trevelor?"

"We will arrive on the morning of the fourth day." He smiled at her a little tentatively, as if sensing her disapproval. "And this is the evening of the first day."

"Wasn't it afternoon when we left Driguera?"

"Yes, but I have found that it is an easier adjustment if I keep the ship on my local time. We could have dinner and perhaps an early night?"

Her eyes flicked around the small ship, looking for a bedroom, but all she could see was a seating area. Did it convert to a bed? A single bed? She had a heated vision of what an early night with him could entail before she pulled her thoughts together.

"I would like to do some sewing before I sleep, if that's okay." Not only did her clothes need repairing but she had always been a woman who took pride in her appearance. She carefully avoided thinking about why that mattered more to her now that she had met Inzen.

"Of course. Would you care to eat first?"

Her stomach rumbled as if in response and she laughed. "Now that you mention it, I am kind of hungry."

"You hunger?" He looked as appalled as if she had said she was starving. "Captain Armad should have taken better care of you."

"Calm down, big guy. He did offer us food, but I was too anxious to eat anything."

He still looked upset, but he nodded abruptly.

"I will prepare a meal immediately." He unbuckled his harness and stood up.

"You don't need to, uh, steer the ship?"

He laughed for the first time, a low rumble that made her insides quiver. "No, my letari. The *Flower* will remain on autopilot until we approach Trevelor. You may remove your harness if you wish."

She fumbled at the control but whatever he had done to tighten the straps had changed the settings.

"Can you help me?" Her voice sounded breathless again.

His eyes darkened as he leaned over, his scent surrounding her. His intriguingly textured cheek was only inches from her mouth, and she gave in to a foolish impulse. As he released the straps, she leaned forward and brushed her mouth against his cheek, his skin cool and dry beneath her lips.

He leapt back as if she had branded him with a hot poker, his hand reaching up to cover the place where her lips had touched. Had she offended him?

"Why did you do that?"

Her own cheeks were on fire, but she lifted her chin defiantly. "It was just a kiss. I just wanted to thank you for what you're doing. I'm sorry if it offended—"

"Oh, no. You did not offend me. You would never offend me by touching me."

His dark gaze was so intense that she dropped her eyes, catching a glimpse of his erection straining at his pants as she did so. Her lips curved even as the heat in her cheeks intensified. No, he was definitely not offended.

CHAPTER EIGHT

Inzen awoke long before his ship's lights began to brighten to signify the coming day. He had not been on Driguera long enough for his system to acclimate so he suspected the cause of his wakefulness was the female lying in the bunk beneath him. The previous evening had filled him with a sense of satisfaction but also an immense longing.

Preparing a meal for her and watching her eat fulfilled his need to protect his female. *Not my female*, he reminded himself yet again. But it felt right to provide for her. Unfortunately, watching her eat and hearing her little moans of appreciation and watching her lick those strange, tempting lips had aroused more than his protective instincts. Since there was little he could do to control his unruly shaft, he resigned himself to making the trip with a permanent erection. He only hoped that Jade was not offended by his arousal.

After the meal, she converted the table to her sewing area, starting with the oversized bronze garment. He had tried to interest himself in a book—he read a great deal on space flights—but he kept finding himself watching her instead. She hummed happily as she cut and seamed the material with sure hands. At one point she looked up and smiled at him.

"The shopkeeper was right. This seaming tool is a vast improvement over needle and thread."

"You seem very familiar with the process. Is that your profession on Earth? A seamstress?"

"Not exactly," she said evasively, then sighed and shook her head. "I forget that no one up here cares who I am."

"Is it confidential?"

"No. But my... business is—was—very successful and people tended to act differently once they knew who I was." He could read the sorrow on her face and his tail flicked towards her, seeking to comfort her, but then she pushed away the melancholy. "My sobo—my grandmother—taught me to sew when I was so young I can barely remember learning. I intend to teach my daughter as well."

She bent back over her sewing and he hoped she had missed his guilty start. Lily was already fascinated by Cassie's dressmaking, but he usually attempted to distract her, only too aware of the dangers in the sharp scissors and heated seaming tool. Would Jade be as cognizant of the dangers they represented?

The words rang hollow. This female had followed her daughter into an unknown universe; she would never be careless with her wellbeing. *If Lily is even her child*, he reminded himself.

As the hour grew later, he saw her yawn several times and was about to suggest that they adjourn when she stood up and shook out the garment.

"There." She glanced uncertainly around the ship's cabin. "Is there someplace where I can try this on?"

"The sanitary unit is the only area with a door and it is quite small." He couldn't bear the disappointed look on her face. "If I give you my word as a warrior not to invade your privacy, would you trust me enough to change here?"

She studied him thoughtfully and he found himself holding his breath. When she nodded, a vast satisfaction roared through him.

"I will cover my face."

He dropped his reader and put his hands over his eyes. She gave a startled laugh, and a moment later, he heard the rustle of fabric. It took every ounce of self-control that he had learned as a warrior not to break his vow as he imagined her naked body standing in the middle of his ship.

"Okay, you can look now. Is it all right?"

All he could do was stare at her. The oversized bronze garment had been transformed into a slim jumpsuit. The fabric gathered at each shoulder before dipping between her slight breasts. A matching sash pulled the fabric tight around her slender waist before it swept out into flowing pant legs. The color brought out the golden tone of her skin and accentuated the crystal green of her eyes. Although the cut was modest, this was the first time he had seen her true shape. How he longed to explore every dainty curve.

"You don't like it?" Her face fell, and he realized that he had been staring in silence for far too long.

"I do not have the words to express how much I like it," he admitted. "You are very talented."

She glowed with pleasure at his compliment, but he had spoken only the truth. Over the past year of living with Cassie, he had grown quite familiar with female fashion. He suspected that Cassie's work might be more professional, but Jade had a unique flair all her own.

"Thank you. It feels much better than my ripped-up clothes—" Her words were interrupted by an enormous yawn.

"It is time for sleep," he said firmly.

"I'm not sleepy—" Another yawn stopped her, and she grinned at him. "I guess I am kind of tired. I had intended to make myself a nightgown, but I suppose the medical gown will do."

She looked so regretful that the offer emerged before he could stop himself. "Would you like one of my shirts to sleep in?"

"Umm, that would be nice."

He rummaged through his locker, pulling out the shirt he used for training. It was designed to cling so perhaps it would not be as voluminous on her as his other garments would be. When he stepped closer to hand it to her, his tail came up and caressed her arm. She looked startled and he forced himself to pull away, even though the need to touch her had been building in him the entire evening. Her face cleared, and she reached out and patted his tail. He tried not to groan as the feeling of her small fingers on the sensitive flesh sent a spike of arousal straight to his shaft. The serenity on her face made it only too clear that she had no idea what she did to him whenever she touched him like that.

"Thank you." She smiled up at him. "Would you mind closing your eyes again so that I can change?"

Instead, he whirled away from her, trying to force his unruly body under control, but the soft whisper of fabric made it impossible.

"All done. Would you mind showing me how to use your bathroom?"

"I apologize. I do not have a bathing room here on the ship." Although he could only too clearly envision her surrounded by the steaming waters of his home pool.

"I didn't expect you to—I meant your place to, umm, get clean?"

"Ah, you mean the sanitary facility." He opened the door to

the tiny unit and ran through the instructions, trying desperately to ignore the warmth of her body against his side and her delicious fragrance swamping his senses.

"Thanks. I think I understand."

They stared at each other for a moment, but she didn't move. Was she going to kiss him again? But then she put a hand on his tail and gently removed it from around her waist. Fuck! Why couldn't he stop touching her?

"I don't think it's large enough for two." She laughed, but the sound was breathless and he could detect the increased scent of her arousal. He forced himself to step back.

"If you need assistance, please call for me. I will keep my eyes closed," he added quickly.

Pink flushed her cheeks before she smiled at him and ducked inside the small compartment. Trying in vain not to listen to the sound of water or imagine her naked body glistening with liquid, he went to change the seating area into two bunks. He usually slept in the lower bunk, but he suspected that the top bunk would be too tall for her to reach. Although he could easily imagine his hands spanning her tiny waist as he lifted her into it, he decided she would be more comfortable on the bottom as long as she didn't mind being beneath him.

That thought immediately raised the image of her beneath him in other ways, and his overanxious cock jerked again. By Granthar, he was worse than a rutting young animal. He sat down at the table and started reciting the words of the warrior's code silently in an attempt to regain control—a control that vanished completely as soon as she emerged from the san.

Her hair was still damp, clinging to the delicate bones of her head and making her eyes look even larger. His shirt hung off one shoulder, revealing her fragile collarbone, and the hem came down below her knees but didn't conceal the graceful golden curves of her calves. She had been lovely in the outfit that she made but seeing her like this—small and vulnerable and wrapped in his clothing—made his chest ache.

"I guess I'm ready for bed."

"I thought you would prefer the bottom bunk."

"If you're sure." She eyed the top bunk a little doubtfully. "I think I would need a boost to get in there."

"No, you take this one. I will be just fine on top."

A startled glance came his way, and he wondered if human females used that expression in regard to sexual positions. Since he could not ask her, he kept his face as blank as possible and went to take his own turn in the san. As he walked past her, she put her fingers on his arm and went up on tiptoes. Unable to resist, he bent his head, and once again those impossibly soft lips brushed across his cheek.

"Thank you again, Inzen. For everything."

Afraid to speak in case he blurted out an offer to give her anything she wanted, he simply inclined his head and went to attend to his needs. When he had emerged, she was curled up in the bottom bunk, her small body barely visible beneath the blanket. He dimmed the lights, leaving only a faint glow in case she needed something during the night, and went to bed.

But he had not slept well and now he found himself awake and restless, long before it would be time to get up. If he had been on his own, he would have risen and spent an hour training in what he already suspected would be a futile attempt to put his mind and body at ease. Since that was not an option, he succumbed to his urges and dropped the hand to his aching cock.

He did not want the touch of his own hand. He wanted Jade's soft small fingers caressing him, but even imagining that made him stiffen further, precum already pearling at his tip. He stroked his thumb through the heated fluid and imagined that it was her tongue—that impossibly smooth soft tongue—tasting his seed. His sack tightened as he imagined her taking him in her mouth as he had imagined it earlier. The forbidden nature of the act was less important than the image of her looking up at him, green eyes wide with pleasure as she swallowed around him. His seed was leaking faster now, and he slipped his hand up and down his cock, imagining her taking him deeper, lightning streaking through his veins until he exploded, his breath escaping in a hoarse gasp.

He had barely begun to soften when he caught the rustle of movement beneath him and his shaft responded immediately, as hard and aching as if he had never come at all. He sighed silently. Only one thing would ease his arousal, and he would never press his attention on a female who was a passenger on his ship, let alone one that he was coming to… care about.

With another silent sigh, he closed his eyes and pretended to sleep once more.

CHAPTER NINE

Jade held her breath and tried not to move as she listened to the faint sounds overhead. The ship had still been in darkness when she awoke, and she had been lying there pondering the circumstances under which she found herself when she heard what sounded like flesh sliding against flesh. A fresh wave of that spicy scent that already permeated the small ship had an unnerving effect on her body as she realized that Inzen was touching himself. Her own hand slipped between her thighs, beneath his shirt, and found an answering wetness. She brushed cautiously against her swollen clit just as she heard him gasp quietly. A moment later, she heard him settle into place. Damn. If she had been able to hear him, he would no doubt be able to hear her if she continued to touch herself. Reluctantly, she withdrew her fingers.

What was it about this big alien that aroused feelings she thought she had put behind her? *It's just been a long time*, she reminded herself. And he was very attractive. Even though he was obviously older than the Cire warriors who had initially recovered her—his ridges more pronounced, the patterns of his skin more complex—his body showed few signs of age.

A pleasant shiver traveled over her as she remembered those impressive muscles. He cut a fine figure in his tight-fitting uniform, but when he came out of the bathroom ready for bed, he had removed his shirt, and she could see every well-defined ridge and bulge as she peeped at him from under her eyelashes. And when he had climbed into the bunk over her, she had another clear view of the even more impressive bulge between his legs. She remembered the small nubs that covered his skin and wondered if they covered his penis as well. An excited little throb jolted her clit at the thought.

No, she told herself. *You don't need this type of complication.* She was here to find her daughter, and no man—no *alien*—no matter how attractive, would get in the way of that. Inzen was only an emissary to help her search, and nothing more.

Despite her resolution, she continued to think of him as something considerably more until at last the ship's lights brightened. From the alacrity with which he climbed down from the bunk, she suspected that he hadn't slept any more than she had, but she ignored the memory of his activities and gave him a pleasant, neutral smile.

"Good morning. At least I assume it is morning?"

"Yes, my letari. And it is a very good morning with you here on my ship." He smiled down at her, his face soft.

Oh lord, if he kept saying things like that, it would be very difficult to maintain any distance between them. She forced herself to look away from both his smiling face and his very tempting body.

"I'm eager to get started on more sewing. Do you mind if I take over your table again?"

"Not at all. But I will prepare the morning meal first."

"I don't usually eat breakfast."

He looked horrified. "You need to keep up your strength. I will prepare a variety of dishes so you may find something that appeals to you."

She opened her mouth to protest but he had already disappeared into the bathroom. Yep, definitely going to be hard to keep her distance.

That thought continued to plague her throughout the morning. First, when he presented her with at least ten different dishes and watched anxiously as she tried a bite of each of them. Then again, when he seemed quite content to sit in his chair and read while she sewed, but she felt him watching her.

For lunch, he would have prepared an equally vast array, but she firmly told him that a single simple meal would suit her better. She resumed sewing after lunch, but she was feeling increasingly restless. Her last year on Earth had been filled with activities from physical training to contacting her investigators to the business tasks she couldn't delegate. She wasn't used to sitting in one place for an extended period of time. After the third time she stretched and sighed, Inzen frowned at her.

"Is something wrong, my letari?"

"Just restless, I guess. I usually train every day and I'm not used to sitting still for so long."

He studied her thoughtfully. "I also devote part of each day to training. Would you care to join me?"

Did one train with an emissary? It was her turn to study him. Training against someone with his size would be a good test of her skills, she decided, ignoring the shiver of excitement at the thought of being close to that big body.

"Will you close your eyes again? I want to change."

He obeyed immediately, and she hurried to change into her yoga pants and sports bra. She had been unable to repair all of the damage, but they were mainly intact and better suited to exercising then her new clothing.

"I'm ready," she called.

Inzen's eyes snapped open, his dark gaze heating as he inspected her outfit. She was suddenly conscious of the strip of bare stomach between the bottom of the bra and the top of her pants, of the slashes in her pants that she didn't have enough fabric to repair, and of the thin strap she had created to replace the missing shoulder strap.

"That is a most becoming outfit. Is it the customary attire for training on Earth?"

"Not unless you've been abducted by aliens," she said dryly, but she could still feel pleasure warming her cheeks at his obvious approval.

"I am sorry that the Vedeckians took you from your planet, but I am very glad that we met."

"Maybe it was for the best. At least this way I have a chance of finding my daughter."

He opened his mouth, and she waited for him to speak, but in the end, he just shook his head. "It is your turn to close your eyes."

"I don't understand."

"I have a training outfit as well."

"Oh, yes, of course."

She closed her eyes, but curiosity won out. When she heard clothing rustle, she couldn't resist a peek from under her lashes. Her mouth went dry. His back was to her, and he was completely naked. A broad back and strong muscular legs met her eyes, but her gaze was drawn to the round, firm curves of his ass and the tail springing from just above his buttocks. His tail flicked towards her, almost as if it could sense her gaze, and she quickly closed her eyes again.

"I am also ready," he said a moment later.

Oh my. He was still shirtless but he had donned a pair of brief black shorts. They clung to his thick thighs and cupped his massive cock so closely that she could see the texture of his skin through the cloth. As if in response to her gaze, his cock jerked, and she realized that he was indeed fully erect. As far as she could tell, he had been erect since the moment they met. Was that normal for a Cire? They must have—must have *had*, she amended—very happy wives.

"Shall we begin?" Inzen asked, and she dragged her gaze away from his genitals.

"Yes. Can you show me your moves?" Ignoring the unintentional double entendre, she gave him a bright smile.

To her surprise, he started by walking her through a series of poses that were very similar to her yoga routine. For a male of his size, he moved with astonishing grace. Despite the fluidity of the positions, she could feel her muscles stretch and burn satisfyingly. By the time they were finished, she was breathless, glowing, and smiling.

"That was a great workout."

"Is it similar to what you practice? You did very well."

"Not exactly but it had some resemblance to what I usually do."

He insisted on waiting until she had replenished her fluids and then studied her again, his head cocked to one side.

"Do you wish to continue?"

"Of course." Jade arched a brow. "I've also studied martial arts."

"I am not surprised, my letari. Your moves on Driguera indicated training." He hesitated. "Would you care to spar? I will not hurt you."

She lifted her chin. "You don't need to worry about me. I can take care of myself."

"Very well."

He bowed and they moved into position. She was immediately aware that this might not have been her best idea. Even though she knew she had been well trained, he was not only larger and stronger but surprisingly fast. Their first bout was embarrassingly short, even though she was sure he had been taking it easy on her. She lasted longer the second time, but she still suspected that he was only playing with her. The third time, she remembered the advice of her favorite instructor, a former streetfighter. *"Use whatever advantage you can find,"* he would say. She realized that every time she moved closer to Inzen, he hesitated for a fraction of a second, perhaps because he was afraid to hurt her.

On her next move, instead of evading his grip, she deliberately pressed against him, her breasts smashed against his hard chest and her stomach against that ever-present erection. He froze and she shifted her weight, taking advantage of his hesitation to slip her leg between his and use his weight to throw him to the mat. Before she could dance away, his shock wore off and he took her down with him, rolling so that she was pressed against the mat and he was looming over her, every inch of that big body pressed against hers.

Her mouth went dry.

"That didn't go the way I expected," she panted.

"You did very well, my letari. It has been many years since a warrior surprised me in training."

His tail curved around and caressed her cheek, an oddly comforting gesture, but then it continued downward, brushing against her collarbone as it moved lower, and that wasn't comforting at all. She squirmed restlessly and felt his cock respond before he murmured an apology and started to lift off of her. As he did, his tail slipped even lower and curled around her breast, tugging gently at her nipple. Her bare nipple. In the flurry of moves, her makeshift shoulder strap had come undone, leaving her completely exposed to his touch.

He looked as shocked as she felt but his tail continued to work the taut bud and, oh, Lord, did that feel good. Her body arched into his touch before she could stop herself.

"It has been even more years since I responded to a female this way," he murmured, his eyes focused on her breast. His big hand came up, lifting the small mound higher, and then his tail was gone, replaced by the hot, shocking wetness of his mouth. The rough surface of his tongue sent waves of pleasure straight to her clit as he licked and sucked desperately at the needy flesh.

A distant part of her brain tried to remember why this was a bad idea, but the need surging through her body made thinking impossible. How long had it been since someone touched her? And had anyone ever focused on her so completely—as if she were the only other person that existed?

He switched to her other breast but his hand remained, working her damp peak with the same intensity. His tail wound between her legs, and she thought she should have been shocked, but the thick length felt amazing as it slid against her damp flesh. Her naked flesh, she realized a second later as his tail parted her lower lips. Her pants were now halfway down her thighs but any impulse to protest disappeared as he found the entrance to her pussy. The tip of his tail slipped inside and she cried out, her hands clamping down on Inzen's broad shoulders.

He lifted his head, his eyes anxious. "Is it too much?"

"God, no." Strange and shocking and wonderfully thick but definitely not too much. She could feel the small nubs that covered his skin rubbing against every sensitive inch as he worked his way deeper inside.

"You are very tight, my letari," he growled, his voice strained. "You are sure this is not uncomfortable?"

Uncomfortable? With a growl of her own, she grabbed those perfect butt cheeks and tried to yank him closer. As she did, her legs parted even further and the full width of his tail pressed against her clit, the textured surface sending shivers of pleasure down her spine. His spicy musk surrounded her, somehow adding to her excitement, and her whole body was on fire with longing, perched on the razor's edge of climax.

"I need more," she panted, writhing against him as she sought that elusive peak.

His eyes darkened, black flames dancing in his intense gaze, and then his huge hand was on her butt, lifting her into his touch as his tail drove deeper. His mouth clamped down on her nipple, the sharp nip of his teeth on the engorged flesh the final touch to send her flying. She clung to him as her body shuddered, waves of pleasure rippling through her in gradually decreasing pulses, leaving her limp, drained, and astonishingly content.

CHAPTER TEN

When Inzen felt Jade climax in his arms, a corresponding wave of pleasure swept over him and his seed—his barren seed—erupted in an explosive but ultimately unsatisfying climax. His cock barely softened despite the copious liquid now bathing both his thighs and hers, and he was suddenly, appallingly conscious of what he had done.

He raised his head, half expecting to find her looking at him with anger, or even worse, fear, but instead she opened her eyes and gave him a lazy, satisfied smile.

"I apologize," he began.

"You don't know how much I—wait, what?" she said simultaneously.

"You are a guest on my ship. I should not have taken advantage of you."

"I don't remember asking you to stop." The smile had disappeared, and she frowned up at him. "Do you think I would have let you do that if I didn't want you to?"

"It is my job to look after you."

"And I'm a grown woman who is quite capable of looking

after myself. But if you're that worried about it, take your tail out of my pussy!"

She shoved at him with her small hands and he realized that he was still buried in the luscious depths of her body. He tried to pull free, but his tail resisted before finally leaving her in a long, slow glide that made her eyes flutter shut. The sweet scent of her arousal filled the small cabin, and he couldn't help licking the glistening evidence now coating his tail. His own eyes closed as her delicious taste filled his mouth and he opened them to find her watching him thoughtfully, no longer frowning.

"For someone so quick to offer up an apology, you look like you're enjoying the results." Her delicate brow arched up.

"You taste sweeter than the first grazen berries of summer," he said honestly as he forced himself to sit back.

Unfortunately, that only exposed more of her tempting body. He could see the marks of his mouth on her small, dark nipples and see the flushed, wet folds of her cunt. His eyes focused there as he realized for the first time just how small she was in comparison to him. And yet, she had taken his tail. Not only taken it, but asked for more.

Without conscious direction, his finger traced the delicate flesh, so unlike that of a Cire female. He didn't find that a lack, especially when he discovered a small pearl of flesh above her entrance. Her whole body quivered when he caressed it with an exploratory finger.

"Inzen!" she gasped, lifting into his touch.

"What is this, my letari? A pleasure receptacle?"

"That's my clit and if you don't stop touching it, you're going to be apologizing again. I thought you didn't want to touch me." She made an adorable attempt to look fierce even as her pearl hardened beneath his fingers.

"Not want to touch you? Touching you pleased me so much that I disgraced myself."

Her eyes flew to his, then down to his wet shorts and the rigid bar of his cock. Her lips curved.

"Then I don't understand. Why did you apologize?"

"Because you are a guest on my ship and... we have a more important purpose."

Her face clouded over, and the reminder put a damper on his own arousal. He reluctantly withdrew his hand and started to help her dress again, but she waved him away.

"I think it would be safer for both of us if I got dressed on my own." She looked ruefully at the tattered remnants of her outfit. "Scratch that. I'll take a shower and put something else on, then see if I can mend these. Again."

"I am sorry."

"Don't be. It was... nice to be touched again." Her hand brushed his tail for the briefest instant before she disappeared into the san.

As soon as the door closed behind her, he groaned, frustrated, aroused, and shocked. Despite his overwhelming attraction to her, he hadn't realized that his need for her would sweep away every particle of control. But when she responded to him so eagerly, her sweet body rising to his touch, all he could think about was pleasing her. And himself, he admitted. If he hadn't regained his senses, he would have buried himself in her hot, tight little cunt. What's more, he suspected that he would have knotted inside her—the sign that a Cire had found a true mate, the one who would cause his seed to become fertile.

A fleeting pang of regret passed through his mind. He had cared for Aria—his first mate—but the feelings he had for her paled in comparison to his feelings for Jade. When she was in his arms, his tail wrapped around her, her sweet, spicy fragrance filling his head, he felt complete in a way he had never experienced before. He suspected that if they were to be mated, it would not be the calm, peaceful relationship he had enjoyed with his first mate. Jade had a streak of fire that befitted a warrior and he could see passionate clashes in the future.

The thought did not displease him. Instead, his cock throbbed eagerly at the thought.

Stop that, he ordered himself. She is a human and she will want to return to her planet. There is no future between us.

Despite his admonishments, when she emerged from the san, clean and sweet-smelling, a shy smile on her face, a future with her was all he could think about. If she did turn out to be Lily's mother, he could have a daughter and a mate. Or he could lose both.

He would have to woo her, he decided. He would be patient and show her that he was interested in more than her tempting body. So much had been taken from him. Surely Granthar would not begrudge him these hopes for a brighter future.

Steeling his resolve, he did his best to ignore the tempting picture she made as he ducked past her to perform his own cleanup. Afterwards, he prepared the evening meal, carefully choosing the items she had shown a preference for earlier that day. Several times during the meal, she shot him an uncertain look, and he suspected she was still thinking about his apology. But he could not bring himself to discuss the matter further when he was already so tempted to repeat the encounter.

When she frowned at her sewing after the meal, he searched for a better way to entertain her.

"Do you enjoy games of strategy?" he asked.

"I used to play chess in college but somehow I suspect I'm not going to find that up here."

"There is a game I enjoy called baduka. Would you care to play?"

"You want me to play with you?" she teased, running her eyes over his body. Before he gave in to the promise in her eyes, she laughed. "Why not? Show me what you've got, big guy."

Ignoring his once again stiff erection, he brought out the baduka game. A simple enough game with black and white markers, the challenge came from the skill of the players. He was not surprised to find that Jade caught on quickly and was soon challenging him with every play. After he won the first two games, she managed to maneuver him to a tie in the third, crowing with delight when he agreed to the draw.

"That was a lot of fun. Thank you, Inzen." She yawned and stretched. "I guess it's time to turn in. Are you going to tuck me in?"

His mouth went dry as she slipped away to change into her —into *his*—shirt for sleeping. He converted the bench back to a sleeping area, then stood uncertainly by her bunk, still not sure about whether or not she had been teasing him.

"Did you wish me to tuck you in?" he asked when she reappeared.

"I would love that, but I think maybe you'd better not." She reached up on tiptoes and brushed an impossibly soft kiss across his mouth. "Good night, Inzen. Sleep well."

All hope of sleep abandoned him, but he dutifully turned out the lights and climbed into his lonely bunk.

JADE TOSSED FROM ONE SIDE OF THE BUNK TO THE OTHER. It was a large bunk, sized for a Cire warrior, but she couldn't find a comfortable position. Her breasts ached, and there was a constant throbbing pulse from her clit. The interaction with Inzen earlier that afternoon seemed to have reawakened all of her sexual desires. Why here? Why now?

It had been so, so long. As soon as she found out that the

last of the many procedures she had undergone resulted in her pregnancy, that had been all she could think about. Nathan had been quite willing to leave her alone in her daze of happiness. She had suspected that he might have found another interest, but she had been content to let him go his own way while she concentrated on her miracle pregnancy. It was only after Hana was born that she became determined that they would be a true family. Her daughter deserved a father, and she had done her best to make Nathan a part of their daughter's life.

And look how well that worked out, she thought bitterly.

The search for her daughter had consumed her life for the past year, and there certainly hadn't been any room for male attention. Was her attraction to Inzen simply a result of the fact that she finally felt like she was making some progress and could relax enough to experience attraction again? It was a comforting theory, but she knew it wasn't the whole truth. Since the moment their eyes had met across the medical bay, she had been inexplicably drawn to him.

Inzen adjusted his position in the bunk above her, and she suspected that he was just as restless. What kind of father was he? Inzen saw to her safety, worried over her eating habits, and taught her new exercise routines and games with seemingly endless patience. If he treated his daughter with the same sort of consideration, she was a lucky girl.

He moved again, and she caught the faintest hint of what sounded like skin against skin. Was he touching himself again? The thought caused an answering spike in her own arousal and she heard him give a little groan.

This was ridiculous. They were both consenting adults. There was no one around to watch or judge. Even though she suspected that pursuing their mutual attraction would make the inevitable need to part more difficult, she didn't want to miss this chance to be with him now. She slipped out from under the covers and stood up.

Her head only barely topped the mattress, but it was enough to see his entire naked body. His very erect naked body. His cock strained towards the ceiling, his big hand wrapped around it as he gave it a long hard pull.

"Do you need some help with that?" She tried to sound sultry but suspected it came across as breathless and eager instead.

Inzen jerked up into a sitting position, banging his head on the ceiling of the bunk as he snatched for the covers.

"I... I apologize."

"Stop apologizing! It's really not necessary." She gathered her courage and offered him her hand. "May I join you?"

He looked at her as if she were offering him the moon on a silver platter.

"Are you sure, my letari? I would be happy to share my bunk with you, but I do not think I have enough control not to touch you."

"Good. Because I have every intention of touching you."

A second later, she was flying through the air as he lifted her effortlessly on top of him, pulling her against his chest, his very firm, muscular chest. His tail wrapped around her waist as his arms came around her, and even though she could feel his erection throbbing against her stomach, he seemed content just to hold her.

"I dreamt of this last night," he whispered finally. "Of having you in my arms."

An unexpected lump formed in her throat. It would be far too easy to become attached to him. She suspected that she already was, but she did her best to remember that this was just a temporary fling.

"Is that what you were thinking about?" she asked lightly,

smiling up at him. "Because it sounded like you had more... carnal thoughts."

"You heard me?"

He looked so shocked that she couldn't resist the impulse to lean up and brush her lips against his.

"Yes. And I liked it." Her hand slid down between them as she finally touched his cock. "But I think I'll like being part of it even more."

The black flames appeared in his eyes again as he cupped the back of her head and pulled her to him to return the kiss. But he was not satisfied with the gentle brush of their mouths—he parted her lips, his tongue plunging deep, and she could feel the textured surface rubbing against her softer flesh. Beneath her fingers, his cock too was textured, hundreds of little nubs tantalizing her as she tried to close her hand around him. He was too large for her to grasp completely, but she did her best to tighten her grip and pull upwards the way she had seen him touch himself.

He groaned into her mouth, his kiss even more demanding as he rolled her onto her back, covering her with his big body. A flash of anxiety assaulted her but then she took a deep breath, letting his comforting scent fill her lungs, and wrapped her free hand around his neck. The ridges that covered his skull continued down his neck and she stroked her hand along them. He shuddered.

"Are they sensitive?" she asked.

"They should not be. They are intended for defense, but when you touch me, it is like trickles of fire down my spine."

"Is that a good thing?"

"Oh, yes, my letari. I could find satisfaction just from your sweet hands on my flesh." The heat in his eyes intensified. "But I want more. I want to be inside you."

CHAPTER ELEVEN

Y*es.*
Jade's immediate reaction to Inzen's blunt words was a definite affirmative. This was why she had come to him, and her pussy gave an eager little throb, but she forced herself to be practical.

"Umm, I need to ask. Do your people carry sexual diseases?"

"It is not something I have ever heard about."

"Really?"

"It is usually... unsatisfying to have sexual intercourse with anyone except our chosen mate," he said, his gaze oddly intent.

"Oh." Did he not want this? From the feel of the massive erection pressing against her stomach, it seemed unlikely. "I thought you enjoyed what we did this afternoon but if you're not interested..."

"My letari, I am quite sure you can feel my interest. Did I not just say that I wanted to be inside you?"

He rocked gently beneath her, and she almost moaned with pleasure. "So, unusual but not impossible?"

He hesitated for the barest fraction of a second. "I am quite sure that I will find pleasure with you. In fact..." He hesitated again.

"In fact, what?"

"I suspect that if I come inside you, my cock will knot—it will swell and lock us together."

Oh my. Why was that thought so exciting?

"I'm okay with that," she whispered, sure her cheeks were turning red.

"That will also cause my seed to become fertile," he added, watching her face. "That means that there is a possibility of pregnancy."

"But we're not the same species." A sudden pang of longing swept over her, and she couldn't hide her bitterness. "And it wouldn't make any difference. I can't have children."

"You have a daughter."

"I do, and it took me ten years and hundreds of thousands of dollars and more procedures than I can count to make it happen. Believe me, it's not a risk."

"It has happened," he said slowly. "Between a Cire and a human."

"Trust me. It won't happen with me. I could barely get pregnant with a human man. It's certainly not going to happen with an alien."

The sorrow on his face matched the ache in her heart, and her excitement faded.

"I'm sorry. Maybe this was a bad idea."

"You no longer wish to be with me?"

How could such a stern face look so hurt? She put a reassuring hand on his cheek, stroking the lightly textured surface. "It's not you, Inzen. It's just that the reminder of everything I went through kind of killed the mood."

"Do you wish to regain it?"

"I think it's too late for—oh!"

He lowered his head, nibbling gently at her neck and somehow finding exactly the right spot to send a pleasurable shiver down her spine. She clutched his shoulders, still not quite sure if she should stay but unwilling to push him away. Perhaps she would have done so if he had shown the same hunger from earlier that day, but instead, he proceeded to worship her body with a gentle, persistent enthusiasm that swept away her doubts. By the time his cock pressed against her entrance, she was once again eager for his touch.

"You are sure, my letari?" Despite the strain in his voice, he waited patiently for her answer.

Was she? Yes. She couldn't deny her desire for this male—so different and yet so right.

"I'm sure. I want you, Inzen."

Inzen looked down at Jade, pleased with her response to his touch. The sadness had vanished from her face. Her cheeks were flushed, her mouth wet and swollen. Her nipples were dark, tight buds, and the heady scent of her arousal drifted from her glistening folds. The dark green of his cock formed a shocking contrast to her golden skin, looking far too large for her small entrance.

She took my tail, he reminded himself and pressed against her. His muscles tightened as her body resisted, then she flowered open around him, kissing his cockhead with silken heat. They both groaned and her eyes flew to his, wide and startled.

"More?" He could only manage the single word.

"Oh, yes."

Her hips rose towards him and it took every bit of his self-control not to simply plunge inside her. Instead, he worked his way slowly into the impossibly tight channel until she somehow had taken all of him into her small body. Blunt little teeth clamped down on her plump lower lip.

"Are you all right?"

"So full," she murmured, wiggling as she tried to adjust to him.

He groaned. "Please do not move. I am fighting for control."

Her lips curved. "You mean I shouldn't do this?" Her hips lifted, taking him an impossible fraction of an inch deeper.

"Jade," he groaned.

"Or this?"

Her already snug cunt tightened around him, working his cock in tight little pulses, and all hope of control vanished. He pulled her closer, thrusting wildly, desperately. She met him just as eagerly and he felt her shudder, felt her body tighten, but he was lost to everything except the primitive need to bury himself inside her. He felt the base of his cock beginning to swell as he plunged into her one final time, fire shooting down his spine as his seed finally erupted and their bodies locked together. He heard her cry out, felt her cunt fluttering around him, but all he could do was hold on as triumph filled him. She was his.

Inzen barely slept for a second night but this time, it was by choice. He did not want to miss a moment with Jade. Even after his knot finally subsided, he spent most of the night holding her close, memorizing the feel of her soft body against his, embedding her fragrance in his scent receptacles. But despite his happiness, his thoughts were troubled. He still had not told her about Lily or the fact that he was raising her as his daughter. How could he hope to convince her to become his mate if he kept secrets from her?

A blinking light on his console alerted him to the presence

of a message and he reluctantly separated himself from his female, covering her carefully with a blanket when she sighed at his absence. He went to retrieve the message with mixed feelings. It was undoubtedly from Abby – she had dutifully sent him a message at least once a day to assure him that Lily was doing well. She had been remarkably patient with the number of messages, warnings, and instructions that he sent in return.

The new message contained a small video of Lily splashing happily in her bath, and his chest ached. He missed her so much, but he was growing increasingly convinced that she would turn out to be Jade's daughter. When she smiled up at the person holding the camera, her head tilted to one side and he caught his breath. The gesture reminded him so much of Jade. He froze the image and looked deeper, searching for a resemblance, but their coloring was so very different—Lily's soft brown curls and brown eyes totally unlike Jade's silky dark hair and her startling green eyes—that perhaps the small gesture was only a coincidence.

"What happened?" Jade sat up in bed. "I thought I heard a child."

He knew he should show her the video, but he could not bring himself to do it, afraid of her reaction. He shook his head.

"I do not hear anything." *Now.* It was not a lie, but it was close enough that his conscience tormented him. "Are you ready to break your fast?"

"Mmm." She raised her hands over her head, stretching lazily, and the covers fell away to reveal her naked body. Her small nipples were already hard, and she gave him a seductive smile. "Isn't it too early? The lights aren't even up yet. Why don't you come back to bed?"

"I..." His guilt overrode his desire but before he could come up with some kind of excuse, the lights began to brighten. "It is morning. I will prepare a meal."

Her lips pushed out, more tempting than ever, but he forced himself to ignore her and turn to the cooking area. As he reached for a plate, her soft hands stroked his tail from the base of the spine to the very end and he shivered, his cock thrusting insistently against his pants.

"What a shame. I had plans for you." Warm lips pressed against his back. He almost turned, almost took her in his arms, but then she was gone, the san door closing behind her. What was he going to do? As much as his conscience plagued him, he didn't know how long he would be able to resist her.

For the rest of the morning, he did his best, burying himself in the ship's records while she sewed. They ate lunch together and he could feel her watching him, her expression troubled, while he tried to keep up a neutral conversation.

When lunch ended, she looked at him, raising an eyebrow in obvious challenge.

"Do you want to train again?"

He did. More than anything. But he did not trust himself to be so close to her and not give in to his desires.

"I... need to continue working on my records."

"I see." Her face shut down completely, forming a smooth, impenetrable mask.

He knew he shouldn't ask, but... "What do you see?"

"It was all a trick, wasn't it? You pretended to be interested in me, to make me feel like you could care for me, but all you wanted was to fuck a human female."

"No! I do care for you. I think that you are my—" He stopped himself just in time. "I never thought to take advantage of you."

Her face softened a fraction. "Oh yeah? Then why were you all over me yesterday but you're trying to avoid me today?"

"I am not trying to avoid you. I am trying to control myself."

"Is that a new way of saying, 'It's not you, it's me?'"

Her voice was skeptical, but he nodded eagerly. "That is correct. I am wrestling with my own problems."

"So you aren't regretting what we did? You still find me attractive?"

"Attractive? You are the most beautiful female I have ever seen." He heard the truth in his words as he spoke and felt a fleeting pang of guilt for his first mate, but he could not deny the truth. He had never felt this way before—so alive, so passionate, so... young. It was as if he had truly discovered mating for the very first time.

Her mask shattered and he could see both hope and disbelief in her eyes. How could he have been so thoughtless? He had never intended to make her doubt herself. With a muttered curse, he shoved his chair back and scooped her up in his arms, carrying her to her bunk and stripping her clothes away before he laid her down.

"Never doubt that I find you beautiful," he growled. "Every part of you is beautiful to me. I love your eyes, so wide and green."

He brushed a soft kiss across her eyelids as her eyes fluttered closed, then drew his lips across her impossibly soft skin to those full tempting lips. He worshipped there, sipping at her delicate flesh.

"Your mouth is as sweet as nillian honey and I could drink from it all day."

Nonetheless, he forced himself to leave the tempting honeypot and descend to her breasts, to the equally tempting peaks, standing proud and waiting for his mouth.

"I love your breasts, so soft and perfect." There, too, he worshipped, switching from one bud to the other until they were hard and glistening and she was straining towards him.

His tail had already been busy between her legs, stroking and teasing the delicate flesh, but he pushed it aside impatiently so that he could taste more of her sweetness, deeper and richer here. He sucked her pleasure receptacle deep in his mouth, circling it with his tongue as it quivered and hardened, while his tail returned, probing impatiently at her small entrance.

"Inzen, please," she demanded, her hands clutching at his shoulders.

His tail plunged deep as he clamped down on her swollen nub. Her body convulsed, rippling around his tail in wave after wave of pleasure as more of her sweetness flooded his mouth. He continued his attentions until at last her body went limp.

Smiling with satisfaction, he moved up next to her and pulled her into his arms.

"Did you find that convincing, my letari?"

"Mmm. If you had been any more convincing, I don't think I'd be able to move for a week."

"And I would be content to remain here with you."

CHAPTER TWELVE

"What was your mate like?" Jade asked softly. They were still curled together in the lower bunk, her body tucked against his.

"Aria?" He thought back over the years. Although he had been hurt by her death, he had a child to care for and had coped by pushing the memory of his mate aside and focusing on his daughter. "She was very kind," he said at last. "And very quiet. But she was very delicate, and she was one of the first taken."

"She sounds wonderful," Jade said, but he could hear the strain in her voice. His arm tightened around her shoulders. "How did you meet?"

"It was at a party. We Cires used to enjoy a lot of parties. When we were introduced, my tail flicked towards her and we knew that we would be mates."

She lifted up on one elbow. "Is that what it means? When your tail is always touching me?"

The aforementioned appendage circled her waist and

tugged her back down. "It is an indication of interest," he said finally.

"But it's more than just a friendly gesture, isn't it? Why didn't you tell me?"

"Because I did not want to frighten you. And perhaps also because I enjoy having your hands on me." Her body relaxed, and he quickly changed the subject. "What was your mate like?"

"He was... not kind." She sighed. "I shouldn't say that. He wasn't unkind. He was just uninterested in anything that didn't benefit him. He wanted money and he wanted to be successful and those were the only two things that really matter to him."

"Not you? Or your daughter?"

"He was interested in me at first, but now I wonder how much of that was because of my family. I thought he didn't know about them when we met but later, I realized that he knew exactly who I was."

"He should have appreciated you for the amazing female that you are."

"You're very sweet, but I'm not sure that I was that amazing back then either. I wanted to be successful too. My grandmother built our company from nothing and I always felt like I had to live up to her."

"She pressured you?"

"Oh no. She loved me very much and she wanted me to be happy. But my mother ... She wasn't interested in the business or in me so I spent most of my time with my grandmother even before my parents died. I grew up admiring everything she did. So the fact that Nathan was ambitious didn't bother me."

"But something changed?"

She sighed and nestled her head deeper into his shoulder. "I decided I wanted to have a baby. And it didn't work. And every year I got older, and every year I didn't get pregnant, and every year Nathan and I grew further apart. It was even worse when I started going through all the tests and procedures trying to get pregnant. He went along with it, but it was obvious he had lost interest and didn't understand why it mattered to me."

"A true mate would value your happiness over anything else."

"Which probably proves that we weren't true mates."

Her admission sent a wave of happiness through him, even though he had no right to be jealous of this unknown male.

"But you eventually succeeded in giving birth, correct?"

"I did, and I was so happy. I foolishly expected that Nathan would be happy as well, but he really wasn't interested. I should have realized that it was impossible to make someone care, but I was determined that Hana would have a real father. The day she was abducted, I had insisted that he take her for a walk so they would have some time together."

Wetness touched his skin, and he realized that she was crying.

"Do not blame yourself. You did not know what would happen."

"How can I not? If it hadn't been for me, she wouldn't have been there. And he wouldn't have died." He gathered her closer as her sobs increased. "The worst part is that I don't know what happened to her—if she's happy or safe or if someone is abusing her."

Her sobs tore at him and he realized that he had no choice. He had to put her mind at ease.

"Jade, please stop crying. I am sure that she is safe and happy and well."

Her head rose, green eyes drenched in tears. "What do you mean? How can you know that?"

"The first Vedeckian ship was intercepted as you were told. I believe that your daughter is one of the two female infants that were on that ship. In fact, I suspect that she is my…" Inzen paused to take a breath. "She is the child that I have been raising as my daughter for the past year."

"What!?" She sprang to her feet and he forced himself not to try and prevent her. "Why didn't you tell me?"

"I was not sure." The words sounded weak, even to himself.

"But you should have told me anyway."

"I know I should have told you. At first, I did not want to believe that it was true because I could not face the thought of losing my daughter."

"She's not your daughter! She's mine."

The words sliced through his chest. "And when I finally faced the truth, I did not want you to look at me the way you are looking at me now."

"Like you betrayed me?" Her bitter laugh made his heart ache. "Because you did. You knew she was everything that mattered to me, and you kept quiet because of *this*?" She gestured between them. "So you could seduce me? So you could brag that you had your way with a human female?"

"Because I care for you and I could not stand the thought of anything coming between us. I had hoped that if Lily turned out to be your daughter, perhaps the three of us—"

"You seduced me so that could keep my daughter?"

His guilt made him hesitate a fraction too long. "No! I told you. I care—"

"If you really cared for me, you would have told me."

She snatched up his shirt, then angrily discarded it and picked up one of her own outfits before disappearing into the sanitary unit.

He forced himself not to go after her, remaining frozen on the bed. His chest ached and he rubbed it absently, knowing that he only had himself to blame. For one fleeting moment, he had thought he had everything. Now he was going to lose it all.

Jade headed for the bathroom and stepped under the shower, determined to wash away Inzen's traitorous touch. Why hadn't he told her that "his" daughter was human? He knew how worried she was about Hana.

He had seemed so sweet and caring and it had all been an act. How many times would it take before she learned? From her first boyfriend in college, who had wanted the reputation of popping the rich girl's cherry, to her husband, who had seen her as a rung on the ladder of success, everyone seemed to have an ulterior motive. But this one hurt most of all.

When Inzen touched her, she truly believed that he cared. She cranked up the heat until the water almost burned her skin, but she could still feel his hands and that tantalizing tail caressing her skin. A tear threatened to escape, but she refused to let it fall. Her grandmother had never believed in giving into sorrow and neither did Jade. By the time she finally stepped out of the shower, her armor was firmly in place.

At least that's what she thought until she stepped out of the bathroom and saw Inzen watching her, sorrow in every line of his big body, but she refused to acknowledge him. Instead, she picked up her sewing supplies and set to work.

He didn't attempt to speak to her, although he silently presented her with food when dinnertime came. Her inclination was to ignore it, but starving herself wouldn't prove anything. After choking down a few reluctant bites, she buried herself in her work again. When the lights dimmed, she crawled into her bunk—wearing the nightgown she had made for herself rather than his shirt—and resolutely closed her eyes.

She heard him prepare for bed, heard him pause next to her bunk.

"Good night, my—good night, Jade," he said softly but she didn't respond. As he climbed into the upper bunk, a single tear escaped and trickled down her cheek.

CHAPTER THIRTEEN

The silence between them stretched on the next morning after Jade awoke. Inzen moved stiffly, his face set in a stern mask but his tail drooped despondently. It flicked towards her whenever she moved, but he always pulled it back, and she was startled to realize how much she had come to enjoy that connection between them.

"We will be landing shortly," he said finally, breaking the silence. "Please take your position and fasten your harness."

As soon as she was seated, he checked the harness, but there was no slow, teasing touch this time. He simply slid his finger beneath the belt strap—but even that sent a wave of unwanted desire through her body. Her breath caught, and she inhaled more of his enticing scent. Their eyes met then, and she could see the regret in his, but the rawness of his betrayal was still too close. She deliberately turned her head away. The merest whisper of breath, too slight to be called a sigh, escaped from his lips as he made a small adjustment to the buckle and withdrew.

He returned to the pilot's chair without speaking but they

were so close in the small cockpit that she couldn't ignore his presence as completely as she wanted. She made herself focus on the planet appearing before them.

Like the pictures she had seen of Earth from space, the surface was covered in swirls of blue and green, but the shades looked very different—the blues edging into purple and the greens ranging from lime to emerald. The planet didn't seem to have any large oceans, but rather many smaller bodies of water interspersed with the land. At least from this distance, it looked beautiful and peaceful, and she could only hope that her daughter had been happy here.

If her daughter *was* here...

No.

She refused to consider the possibility that this was yet another dead end and focused on admiring the planet instead. As the ship flew closer to the surface, she began to pick out even more colors. A wide variety of foliage in an astonishing array of bright colors surrounded low buildings in equally bright shades. Inzen headed for a large landing field.

"I will land the ship here and we will transfer to my personal flyer." Before she could object, he continued, "I have spoken to Abby—one of the human females—and she has arranged for the children to be present to meet you."

The obvious strain in his voice tugged at her heartstrings, and for the first time she found herself considering how difficult this must be for him as well. If he had been caring for her daughter for the past year, she had no doubt that he loved the little girl. Perhaps he could still visit with Hana once she reclaimed her. The idea appealed to her more then she would have liked but her attraction to the big warrior was undeniable.

"All right," she agreed, and saw his shoulders relax a little.

He said nothing else as he brought the ship into a smooth landing, then gathered up her belongings, once again neatly wrapped, before she could protest. Deciding it was a battle not worth fighting, she followed him down the landing ramp. Twice, his tail started towards her, and both times, he yanked it back. She didn't need his assistance so why did she miss the comforting warmth of his tail around her waist?

The landing field on Trevelor was very different from the one on Driguera. Although there was a bustle of activity, there were fewer ships and most of them were small. Instead of being surrounded by multistory buildings, she saw only a profusion of the brightly colored vegetation, which seemed more like enormous grasses than the trees she knew.

A pair of workers hailed Inzen and he threw up a casual hand in response as he kept walking, but she came to an abrupt halt. The two males had feathered crests, one in shades of yellow and orange, the other in every shade of blue, with the feathers descending down over their arms like vestigial wings. They had small, plump bodies and long, thin legs with birdlike feet, and she had never imagined anything like them.

"Is something wrong my—Jade?" Inzen asked, frowning at the workers.

"No," she said, resuming the walk. "I just wasn't expecting bird aliens."

"Ah. The Trevelorians are quite different, but they are a good species. Their civilization was not as devastated by the Red Death and they have opened their planet as a refuge to many other species." He hesitated. "Both Cire and human are welcome here."

She didn't respond as she followed him into his flyer, but her mind was already turning over possibilities. If this were a safe planet, perhaps it would be a good place to settle down with her daughter. And Inzen could come and visit them.

The flyer had a driver's seat at the front and Inzen headed for that as she stepped into the passenger compartment. As she started to sit down, she found a small pink blanket tucked into the seat and unexpected tears filled her eyes. Was this her daughter's? She raised it to her face, pressing the soft fabric against her cheek, and inhaled a mixture of both Inzen's scent and a delicate floral undertone.

"Is this hers? Is this Hana's?"

"It belongs to Lily," Inzen replied, his voice tight.

She didn't ask any more questions but clutched the blanket for the rest of the journey. Inzen lifted into the air, circling around the wide, attractive city before heading out across the countryside.

"I thought you said you lived in town?"

"I do. But there is a Cire colony where Abby and Hrebec live. I left Lily with them while I went to meet you on Driguera."

"Why did you come for me?" The question had been nagging her. "You could have let the patrol ship bring me here."

He stared straight ahead, refusing to look at her, but she saw his tail stirring restlessly.

"I wanted to know. Putting off the knowledge of an unpleasant truth will not make it any less true."

"Unpleasant?" The words caught in her throat. "Is that what I am?"

At her question, he turned to face her, his face shocked. "Never. I can never regret meeting you." His gaze dropped to his hands. "But I do not want to lose my daughter."

My daughter, she wanted to cry, but the pain on his face was something she understood too well.

"Perhaps it will be the other child," she suggested.

"Perhaps. But her parents will suffer just as much."

"Are you trying to make me feel guilty for wanting my child back?"

"Of course not." For the first time since the previous day, he didn't pull his tail back when it reached out to her, curving comfortably around her wrist. "No one is at fault here, except the Vedeckians, of course. It is just a difficult situation."

Her anger faded away, leaving only sadness behind. She turned to look out of the window and he returned to the controls, but his tail remained encircled around her wrist.

When they finally landed, she had a vague impression of rustic, colorful houses with open porches and thatched roofs and neat fields stretching out from a small village, but all she could focus on was the thought that she would soon be reunited with her daughter. Inzen escorted her through the village and she caught a glimpse of more of the colorful Trevelorians, as well as a variety of other aliens, before he came to a halt in front of a larger house overlooking a sparkling river.

Inzen knocked, and a moment later, a human woman answered the door. An attractive woman with dark hair and a warm smile, she looked to be about Jade's age, but she was heavily pregnant. Her throat swelled with familiar envy.

"Hi. I'm Abby, and I'm so, so sorry for what you've been through." Abby's gaze traveled to Inzen. "I'm sorry for both of you."

"Where is she?" She knew she was being impolite, but she didn't care.

"All of the children are out back." Abby's eyes were sorrowful as she studied Jade's face. "Do you think you will be able to recognize her after all this time?"

The question had haunted her throughout their trip, but she refused to acknowledge it. "Of course I will."

Abby opened her mouth as if she was about to say something but simply shook her head and led them through the house. A wide porch ran along the entire back of the building and another Cire warrior was seated there, watching children playing on a big blanket.

"Elaina couldn't stand to be here," Abby said softly. "I promised to let her know."

Jade heard the words, but they didn't mean anything. She was too focused on the children. With the exception of a blonde little girl, perhaps five or six, all of the children looked to be the right age. A little boy and a redheaded girl were bent over a toy, but she passed over both of them immediately. Another little girl was handing a block to a small Cire girl, but she looked up as they came out of the house.

Jade's heart skipped a beat.

Big brown eyes and brown curls—she looked so much like her husband that she knew she had finally found her daughter. The world started to spin around her, and Inzen's tail circled her waist as his arm went around her shoulders.

"It is all right, letari."

She clung to him, tears pouring down her cheeks, as the little girl—as *Hana*—climbed to her feet and toddled towards them, shrieking with joy.

"Dada! Dada!" She threw herself at Inzen. With an uncertain look at Jade, he scooped her up. The little girl gave him a big kiss and then scowled at him. "Dada gone."

"I know, little one. But I brought someone back to meet you."

He turned her to face Jade, but Hana refused to look at her and buried her face in Inzen's neck. His face was agonized, but she forced herself to ignore it as she reached for her daughter.

"Hana? It's me—your mama."

Hana only clung tighter to Inzen.

"She's used to being Lily now," Abby said gently.

Her heart breaking, Jade put a cautious hand on her daughter's back—so small and fragile and yet so much larger than it had been the last time she had touched her. Of course her daughter didn't know her anymore. Along with the sadness, anger burned within her. She had missed so much. First smiles, first steps, first words. Even though it wasn't Inzen's fault, he had been there for all of them, and she glared at him. The tail that had still been around her waist dropped away as he looked from her to the child still clinging to him, despair in every line of his body.

What on Earth—or on Trevelor—was she going to do now?

CHAPTER FOURTEEN

Inzen's chest ached. As happy as he was to have Lily back in his arms, he couldn't stand the devastation on Jade's face. When he saw her sorrow turned to anger, he couldn't blame her, even though he had not been responsible for the loss of her daughter. Lily's arms tightened around his neck, and he gave her a soothing pat before remembering it was no longer his place to do so. But how could he give her up? Aside from the biological facts of her parentage, she was his daughter in every sense of the word.

Jade's hand reached out again, almost tentatively, to stroke Lily's head, and his tail instinctively brought her closer. The three of them, together like this, felt so right. Like a family. The thought sent a wave of hope through him. Was it still possible that the three of them could form a family? That neither of them would have to lose a daughter?

He raised his head to find Abby staring at them thoughtfully. Did she have the same idea? But the one he wished to discuss it with was Hrebec. His former captain was the best person to advise him on how to approach a human female.

"Lily," he said gently, "this is your mama. Wouldn't you like to meet her?"

"No," came the muffled response from his neck.

The look of anguish on Jade's face went straight to his heart.

"Lily, you could show your mama where we keep the cookies," Abby suggested.

That actually resulted in Lily raising her head for a minute, but she looked down at Jade and shook her head. Her tiny arms went back around his neck.

"My dada."

As much as it warmed his heart to hear her say it, he couldn't bear the hurt in Jade's eyes. He reluctantly started to peel away Lily's arms, but Jade shook her head.

"I should have realized that it would take time. Forcing her will only make it worse."

To hell with asking Hrebec's advice. He wanted this resolved.

"Would you care to take a walk with me? With us?" he amended quickly.

"If you think I'm letting her out of my sight, you're entirely mistaken. But I'm willing to walk with both of you."

"We will be back shortly," he said to Abby as Hrebec walked over to join her.

"Of course." Abby hesitated. "Jade, I don't want to question your instincts, but are you sure?"

"Oh, yes. She looks just like my husband." He did not like the reminder of her former mate, but he managed to keep silent as her eyes went to the other little girl. "There weren't any redheads in his family, and certainly not in mine. But I assume we could do genetic testing if necessary?"

"I would recommend it," Hrebec said. "It would eliminate any doubt."

"I want to let Elaina know." Abby turned to Jade. "She and her mate are the ones who adopted Ginger. Mikey belongs to them as well."

Jade tilted her head, studying the other two infants, and Abby shot him a startled look. She too had recognized the gesture.

"I'm very sure," Jade said. "I'm fine with doing the test to make it official, but I don't need it to know."

"She'll be very relieved." Abby bit her lip as she looked at him again. "I'm sorry. I know it's a terrible situation."

He inclined his head, then offered his hand to Jade. Would she take it? Immense relief washed over him when she put her hand on his after a long pause.

As they started to leave, Lily suddenly raised her head.

"Bobo," she demanded.

"Here he is," Abby said quickly, retrieving the toy from the blanket and handing it to him.

Jade's eyes fastened on it, then tears began flowing down her cheeks once again.

"What is it, my letari?"

"The toy..." she whispered, running a finger along the faded fur before Lily seized it. "My grandmother made it for me when I was a baby. I looked for it after Lily was taken, but I couldn't find it."

"It is her favorite," he said softly.

A shaky smile appeared as she watched Lily cuddle Bobo close. "Somehow it makes me feel better to know that she had a part of my family with her all this time, comforting her." She dashed away the tears with an impatient hand. "Let's take that walk."

Together they walked down to the shore of the small river. Multicolored stones in various jewel tones formed a shallow rocky beach, and Lily looked around with interest.

"Down, Dada," she demanded.

They were so close to the water. Was it safe? He hesitated, and Jade frowned at him.

"Aren't you going to put her down?"

"But the water is right there."

"And there are two adults watching her. Do you really think that either one of us would let anything happen to her?"

"I suppose you are right." He reluctantly placed Lily on the ground and she tugged him down after her, putting Bobo on his lap.

"Dada, stay," she ordered as she began inspecting the rocks, shooting frequent suspicious glances at him over her shoulder.

"Will you join me?" he asked.

He held up a hand to Jade, and once again she delighted him by letting him assist her as she sat down next to him. They sat in silence, watching his—*her* daughter playing.

"I have an idea," he said finally.

"Yes?" She gave him a suspicious look.

"I know you do not have any credits—"

"If you think for one second that I would ever sell you my daughter—" she began, her tone furious.

"No, of course not. I was just thinking about the fact that without credits you may find it difficult to arrange for living quarters."

She twisted the ring on her finger she always wore, the one with the stone that matched her eyes. "I thought maybe I could sell this."

"But you said that your grandmother gave it to you and that it had great value."

She shrugged, but he could see the pain on her face.

"Hana is more important to me than any piece of jewelry." Then she sighed. "But maybe I should get used to calling her

Lily. If that's the name she's comfortable with, then that's what really matters."

"Did the name you gave her have significance?"

"It was my grandmother's name." But then she looked up at him, eyes flashing green fire. "But whether I change her name or not, she's still my daughter."

"I recognize that, Jade. I would never try to keep you from your daughter." He reached out and took her hand. "But in every way except birth, she is my daughter too." She started to draw away and he firmed his grip, not hurting her, but not letting her go either. "I wondered if it would be possible for us to share her."

"Share her? You mean like joint custody?" Her head tilted as she considered him, and he hoped it was a good sign that she had not immediately rejected his offer.

"I am unfamiliar with that term. I thought that perhaps we could have a mating contract drawn up and you and Lily could live with me."

"A mate contract?" Her eyes widened. "Are you asking me to marry you?"

"I believe that is the term that Abby uses." She was still staring at him so he hurried on. "I would assert no claim over you, but you would have a place to live and I could continue to see Lily—I mean, Hana, every day."

"What if it didn't work out? What if I wanted to leave? Would you try to keep—" she hesitated, her eyes darting to the little girl picking up rocks "—Lily?"

I would try and keep both of you. But he suspected she was not ready to hear that.

"I would not use it as an attempt to keep her from you," he said finally.

"Look, Dada." Lily came up and dumped a handful of

sandy rocks in his lap. He dutifully admired them and then suggested gently, "Why don't you show them to Mama?"

Lily scowled. He thought she was about to refuse, but then she picked over the small handful and pulled out a green one. She offered it to Jade, although she kept her hand on his knee the whole time.

"Eyes."

"Yes, baby. It does match my eyes. Thank you very much."

Lily nodded a few times before she was overcome by a giant yawn, and she climbed up into Inzen's lap.

"Are you sleepy, little one?"

"Nap," she said and started to put her dirty thumb in her mouth.

Appalled, he pulled out one of the cleansing cloths he always carried and cleaned it thoroughly before letting her continue. Used to his ways, she didn't protest but simply popped it in her mouth as soon as he was through and settled back against him. He looked up to find Jade studying him.

"What?"

"Nothing. I'm just surprised."

"At what?"

She didn't answer him, her gaze going back to the water sparkling across the rocks.

"Very well," she said finally. "I'll agree to this mating contract."

Satisfaction roared through him and his tail immediately circled her waist, pulling her closer. He would like to have kissed her, but he didn't want to take any chances on her changing her mind. Once she was his, he would have all the time he needed to show her how he felt. Instead, the three of them sat in silence and watched the water flow.

. . .

Jade sat next to Inzen, snuggled against him, if truth be told, and tried to sort out her tumbled thoughts. The last twenty-four hours had been such a roller coaster of emotion. First her happiness at being with Inzen shattered by the knowledge that he'd been keeping secrets from her. And then finding her daughter, only to be rejected by the person she loved most in all the world. But as heartbreaking as it had been to be rejected by her daughter, the love between Inzen and Lily was all too clear, and she found herself softening towards him. And now, he was suggesting a marriage of convenience.

It's a practical solution, she told herself. Captain Armad had made it quite clear that she couldn't return to Earth. Right now, she didn't have any way to support herself, and while she had no doubt that she would manage somehow, it would be much easier to have someone assisting her. And not just anyone, but the male that her daughter obviously loved. If nothing else, it would give her time to get to know Hana—Lily—again and for her daughter to get to know her.

What else would this marriage entail? Obviously, they would be living together, but he hadn't mentioned sex. Was he no longer interested? For that matter, was she?

His tail stroked the palm of her hand in what was obviously intended to be a comforting gesture, but the nubs caressing her skin were unexpectedly arousing. The memory of those same nubs covering his cock as he plunged it inside her sent a shiver down her spine, and she felt herself dampen.

Inzen shot her a startled look. "My letari?"

Oh, Lord, could he tell that she was aroused? Ignoring his question, she rose to her feet, brushing off the back of her dress. The new outfit she had chosen so carefully was a little the worse for wear, but she couldn't find it in herself to care. She had her daughter. Even if it took time, she was sure they could rebuild their relationship. And she had what felt like the beginning of something with Inzen. The world seemed a lot brighter than it had this morning when she woke up.

CHAPTER FIFTEEN

"This is your house?"

Jade eyed the bright peach-colored building doubtfully. It was one of many on the busy street, all of them ranging from two to three stories, painted in bright colors and topped with thatched roofs. Shops occupied the first floor of each building and the one in front of them was clearly a clothing store. While the outfits on display were bright and appealing, the window was too cluttered to showcase them properly.

"Yes. I purchased it when we decided to stay on Trevelor. Cassie is a very talented seamstress. She and her daughter occupy the second floor."

He was clearly proud of the woman, and Jade fought back a wave of something that felt uncomfortably like jealousy. That jealousy only increased when the shop door flew open and a tall, slim woman rushed out and threw her arms around Inzen and Lily. Inzen stepped back with a quick look at Jade, but Lily grinned and threw herself into the woman's arms.

Her heart ached. On the trip back to Wiang, Lily had refused to be separated from Inzen. During the procedure to sign the mating contract, she had sat on Inzen's lap and ignored Jade completely. Jade had done her best to hide her hurt as she studied the papers. No matter how much they protected her custody rights, they couldn't make her daughter hug her. Her daughter appeared to have no such reservation about the new woman.

Barely a woman, she realized as the girl turned to face her. Her young face hardened as she studied her with distrust.

"Cassie, this is my mate, Jade. She is Lily's mother."

"You don't look like her."

"No," she agreed, ignoring Cassie's attempt to goad her. "She takes after my husband."

"Yeah? Where's he? Does he know you ran off and mated someone else?"

"Cassie—"

"It's all right, Inzen," she interrupted, leveling a look at Cassie. "He doesn't know because he's dead. He was killed when Hana—when Lily—was abducted."

A flash of sympathy crossed the girl's face before it hardened into a sneer. "So now you've found yourself a rich warrior to take care of you?"

"Just like you did," she snapped, then immediately regretted the words. "I'm sorry. I just meant that this is a new world for all of us."

It was too late. Cassie scowled at her and then turned to Inzen. "We've all missed you. Why don't you and Lily come to dinner tonight?"

"If my mate wishes," Inzen said firmly. "Would that please you, Jade?"

She would rather be nibbled to death by ducks, but she forced a pleasant smile. If they were sharing the house, they would need to get along.

"Sounds delightful." The words came out more sardonically than she intended, and Cassie arched a skeptical brow at her before turning back to Inzen.

"Why don't I keep Lily while you show your... mate your house?"

A spiteful part of her rejoiced when Lily immediately threw herself back towards Inzen.

"Dada!"

Cassie laughed and smiled triumphantly at Jade. "She's such a daddy's girl."

"This way," Inzen said, his tail curling around her waist and steering her to a small gate to one side of the shop that she hadn't noticed before.

"See you in an hour!" Cassie called after them, and Jade looked back to find the girl frowning after them.

"That did not go as well as I had hoped," Inzen admitted as he opened the gate and led her along a gravel path.

"You think? Are you sure she isn't in love with you?"

"I am quite sure. But she was treated poorly on that Earth of yours and she finds it difficult to trust people."

She felt a pang of unwilling sympathy as she thought about her own trust issues.

"I'm sure she'll come around," she said, mentally crossing her fingers, then pushed the thought aside as Inzen opened a second gate to reveal a beautifully landscaped garden. "Oh, this is gorgeous."

A fountain sparkled in the center of the garden, surrounded by a smooth oval of low-cut blue grass. Planting beds filled with flowers and more grasses curved sinuously against the outer walls. The main building formed one end of the garden while a small yellow cottage occupied the other end. Behind a shaded pergola, doors that reminded her of shoji screens lined the front of the cottage.

"Down, Dada," Lily demanded and Inzen obeyed, setting

her carefully on the grass. She toddled off to the fountain, trailing Bobo behind her.

"You need not worry," Inzen said reassuringly. "There is mesh over the water so she cannot fall in."

"Of course there is." He was so protective—perhaps a little too protective—but she couldn't fault his determination to keep her daughter safe.

"Would you like to see our home?"

When she nodded, his tail tightened around her waist, then he led her to the cottage, throwing open the screens to reveal a large, comfortable room with a seating area at one end and a kitchen area at the other. Behind the main room, a short hallway led to a big bathroom and two bedrooms. One bedroom was obviously Lily's, decorated in pink and white and overflowing with toys. In addition to a beautifully crafted crib, a canopy bed looked fit for a princess. The other bedroom was larger, with a massive bed and more screens, these opening out to a little pocket garden in soothing tones of gold and green.

She eyed the bed thoughtfully, then realized that Inzen's tail had slipped down from her waist to stroke lightly across her bottom. Did he assume that now that they were officially mated she would be sharing his bed? Her nipples tightened as she remembered their time together on the ship. She couldn't say she was entirely opposed to the idea—but she also wasn't sure if she was ready to fully embrace him as her husband.

"My letari." Inzen's voice deepened and she looked up to find him watching her, black eyes hungry with desire. Logic disappeared and an answering flare of need had her starting to sway towards him when Lily wailed from the garden.

"Dada! Bobo wet."

He hesitated, clearly torn, and she gave him a gentle push. "Go on. Go rescue Bobo."

. . .

Why the hell did I agree to this? Later that night, Jade scowled up at the canopy of Lily's princess bed and wondered if she made the wrong decision. Dinner had been an unmitigated disaster. Inzen had failed to mention that the top floor of the main house was occupied by TeShawna, another human woman, her Cire mate Mekoi, and their daughter Vanessa. Jade found the fact that TeShawna had taken on the challenge of studying to become a medic on an alien planet with alien patients very impressive and would have loved to talk to her about it. Unfortunately, the other woman had clearly picked up on Cassie's hostility and wanted nothing to do with her.

Cassie either ignored her or made little jabs at her expense, not quite obvious enough for Inzen to pick up on although he obviously sensed the tension between the women. Both he and Mekoi tried to steer the conversation in a neutral direction, but by the time the evening ended, Jade's head pounded and her jaw ached from the fake smiles.

It only got worse when they returned to the cottage. Lily had been thrilled to play with the other little girls, but by the time they got home, she was tired and cranky. She didn't want her bath, she didn't want to put on her nightgown, and she definitely didn't want to sleep in her own room.

"Sleep wif Dada!" she wailed as Inzen gave Jade a helpless look.

"Fine." What was the point in arguing? She hated to see her daughter unhappy, and the long, emotional day was catching up with her. "I'll sleep in Lily's room."

She half-expected Inzen to object but he only studied her face and nodded solemnly.

Now, here she was, alone on a narrow bed and unable to sleep despite her exhaustion. She wished she was snuggled against Inzen's big body but all she could do was hug her pillow. It was a poor substitute but as she finally started to drift off to sleep, she allowed herself to hope that tomorrow would be a better day.

Inzen stared at the ceiling of his room as Lily mumbled in her sleep. He was delighted to be reunited with his daughter, but this was not how he had expected to spend his first night as a mated male. When he had shown Jade the bedroom earlier, he saw the speculation in her eyes and caught the sweet scent of her arousal when she leaned towards him. But then when he was trying to handle Lily's tantrum, she had abandoned them both to sleep in Lily's room. Was she still reluctant to sleep with him after his betrayal?

As much as his body—and his heart—longed for her to join him, he wouldn't rush her. He would wait for her to come to him in her own time. In the meantime, he would do whatever he could to make her happy. As he listened to his daughter—their daughter—settle into slumber, he began to make plans.

The first one he announced at breakfast the next morning. Lily had regained much of her normal good humor, but she still clung to him and avoided Jade. He could see how much it hurt his mate, but he knew it would take time for the little girl to accept her.

"I talked to Cassie, and I thought perhaps you would like to work in the shop with her in the mornings."

"What about Lily?"

"I will watch over her." The uncertainty in her eyes pained him but he understood her fears. "I promise we will be right here in the house or the garden. It would give you an opportunity to earn some credits of your own," he added when she started to shake her head. "Of course you are welcome to everything I have, but I suspect that you would be happier with your own income."

"Cassie agreed to it?" she asked doubtfully.

"She did." *Eventually.*

He and Lily had gone to see Cassie before Jade woke up.

Cassie's first objection had been that she had no money to pay for additional help.

"I thought the shop was doing well?" he had asked.

"It was. At first. But business has started dropping off and I'm not sure why."

"It just takes time, Cassie. And you know I am happy to support the shop as long as necessary."

He had plenty of credits put aside and no qualms about spending them on either of his daughters. Or his mate.

"I will reimburse you for her salary," he promised.

"Does she know anything about clothes? Or sewing?"

"She is a very talented seamstress," he said. When Cassie scowled, he immediately realized he had made a mistake, but he would not deny his mate's talent.

"I guess she can work for me," she finally agreed, but Inzen could tell she wasn't happy.

He decided not to share their conversation with Jade. They were both intelligent, caring women. Hopefully, spending more time together would bring them closer.

CHAPTER SIXTEEN

Jade scowled out into the townhouse garden and wondered yet again why she had agreed to this arrangement. Her first few days working with Cassie had proved to be an unmitigated disaster. Her distrust was so extreme that Jade would have assumed the woman was in love with Inzen if their father-daughter relationship hadn't been so obvious. If anything, Cassie treated her like a wicked stepmother. The fact that Lily obviously loved the other woman only added insult to injury.

Cassie gave her the most menial jobs she could find and refused to let her do any sewing. Jade had tried to make a few tactful suggestions but was shot down every time. The only bright spot had been when Cassie begrudgingly allowed Jade to take some spare fabric so she could make herself some more clothes in the evenings. Despite that, the reason she continued to work in the shop was because the girl was genuinely talented. All of Jade's professional instincts were intrigued, and she wanted her to succeed. She also suspected that if she had any hope of forming a real family with her daughter and Inzen, she and Cassie would have to learn to get along.

But the biggest sources of her frustration were the big warrior and tiny girl playing together in the courtyard garden. Lily was perched on Inzen's back, his tail holding her in place as he crawled around on his hands and knees while she squealed with laughter. She wanted to join them but knew that as soon as she did, Lily's smile would fade.

Her hopes of finding a way into her daughter's heart were also beginning to fade. Lily still regarded her with the utmost suspicion, and it had finally occurred to Jade that she associated her appearance with Inzen's absence. Lily also didn't like it when Inzen's tail touched Jade, snatching it away from her any time it did.

"My dada."

Inzen had allowed it the first few times, but at least he finally put his foot down the last time Lily had tried to pull his tail away from Jade.

"No, little one. Mama is part of our family too."

Lily had scowled but accepted it. Perhaps it was hopeful thinking on Jade's part, but she thought maybe Lily had softened a little bit towards her after that. It certainly hadn't stopped her from demanding Inzen's presence.

Yesterday, they had discussed leaving Lily with Jade in the afternoon while Inzen visited the training school he sponsored, but while Inzen had agreed, Lily had dissolved into a flood of tears when it was time for him to leave. With a helpless look at Jade, he had agreed to take her with him. Determined not to let her daughter out of her sight, she accompanied the pair.

The training school was a long low building, the rooms arranged around several interior courtyards, and it reminded her of the dojo when she had taken some of her martial arts classes. Lily seemed at home there, and none of the fighters seemed surprised by her presence. Inzen's office had a play area with a child-sized tent piled with pillows in one corner, Lily climbed inside, tugging Bobo with her, when Inzen gently but firmly told her that it was nap time.

At least he doesn't let her get away with everything, Jade thought bitterly but immediately regretted the thought. He was a good father, watching over Lily carefully and making sure that she had a standard routine. It was only where Jade was concerned that he seemed reluctant to correct her behavior.

A glass wall formed the front of his office, and as Lily drifted off, he gestured to Jade to step outside with him.

"I hope you do not mind that I allowed her to accompany me," he said anxiously.

"I guess not. I can't bear to hear her cry either."

"It is not just that. I do not want her to blame you for separating us."

She sighed, some of her annoyance dissolving as he echoed her earlier thoughts.

"I suppose I understand. It's just so hard waiting for her to accept me."

"I know, my letari. But we are making progress."

He glanced back through the glass and she followed his gaze. Lily was sound asleep, her thumb in her mouth and her other arm clutching Bobo.

"Do you want to stay with her while I spar?"

"Spar?" The question conjured up an image of their time on the ship, and an unexpected spike of arousal caused her nipples to harden.

"Yes, I have a few private students that I train with."

"*Female* students?" She narrowed her eyes at him and he laughed, his tail wrapping around her waist and tugging her up against his big body.

"No, my letari. You are the only female that I will ever train with."

Her breath hitched as his eyes darkened. Just as he started to lower his head towards her, another Cire warrior appeared.

"Chief Inzen, I was informed that you had returned. Was your trip successful?"

The warrior who joined them was as large as Inzen but had the smoother skin and small ridges that indicated youth amongst the Cire. A terrible scar ran down his face and onto his chest, leaving one eye milky white.

"Yes, Sentu. It was most successful. This is Jade, my mate and the mother of my daughter."

The young warrior courteously bowed his head. "I am pleased to meet you, mate of Inzen." He hesitated. "Have you made your residence with Cassie—with the other members of Inzen's family?"

Interesting. His tone had definitely changed when he mentioned Cassie's name, and she shot a quick glance up at Inzen to see if he noticed. Since he was scowling at the other male, she suspected that he had.

"Yes, we're living in the cottage at the back. Maybe you could join us for dinner one night." She heard Inzen growl softly and felt his tail tighten around her waist so she hurried on. "I mean with the whole family, of course."

"I would be most honored. That is, if you would permit me to join you, Chief Inzen."

For a dreadful moment, she thought Inzen was going to refuse, then he nodded his head. "That would be acceptable. Did you wish to see me about anything else other than wrangling an invitation to dinner?"

The young male's shoulders went back and he spoke stiffly. "I had hoped that we could train together but if it is inconvenient—"

Some of the tension left Inzen's body and he looked down at her. "You will stay with Lily while we train? We will be in that room so she—so you can see us."

He pointed across the hallway to a wide doorway that led into an empty room with padded mats on the floor. A set of matching doors on the far side of the room opened onto one of the interior courtyards.

"That's fine. I'm happy to stay with her."

"I will prepare," Sentu said eagerly as he turned away. As he headed down the corridor, she noticed that he had a definite limp.

"I do not like your eyes on another warrior," Inzen growled.

"You can't possibly think I'm interested in him."

"Because of his injuries?"

"No, you jerk." She glared up at him. "Because he's obviously too young for me, because he's obviously interested in Cassie, and because I'm mated to you."

His tail stroked her arm. "I apologize, my letari. Sometimes my instincts lead me astray. I do not like you watching other males. Or asking them to share a meal. I do not even like them close to you."

Okay, that should not have been as hot as it sounded. She was a strong, independent woman. Sternly ignoring the pleasant tingle of excitement in her stomach, she tried to keep a stern face, but his apologetic look faded and he tugged her closer.

"Perhaps you do not mind my instincts," he murmured.

"Only under certain circumstances."

Her voice sounded breathless even to her own ears. The hard peaks of her nipples rubbed against his chest and she didn't pull back. Despite everything that had been happening, she had missed being with him.

The sound of male voices came from behind him, and he reluctantly stepped back. "Perhaps we can discuss this later."

"Perhaps."

She traced a teasing finger down his chest before she returned to the office. He groaned and went to change while she settled comfortably in his oversized chair. A few minutes later, he and Sentu reappeared in the room across the way. He was wearing the brief shorts that he had worn on the ship and a tight-fitting shirt that showed off every muscle. *Oh my.* She remembered what it was like to touch every inch of that impressive body, and her lingering arousal spiked again.

Sentu wore a similar outfit, and she could see that his muscles were just as impressive, despite a wicked scar that ran the full length of one leg. What had happened to the young warrior?

The two males began the same exercises that Inzen had shown her on the ship but moved through them with astonishing speed. She could tell that Sentu didn't have the same fluidity to his movements, but he never hesitated. When they finished the final position, they turned to face each other.

Both males bowed, and then Sentu's foot lashed out and the bout began in earnest. They were better matched than she had anticipated. The younger male was surprisingly fast in spite of his injuries, although Inzen was clearly stronger and more experienced. Her pulse pounded as Inzen's big, muscular body strained against the younger male's before flipping him to the mat. He reached down to help Sentu up, obviously lecturing him, and then they began again. Her training had been sufficiently thorough to understand the skill involved in their bout and she watched their moves in fascination.

"Dada?" A small hand tugged on her leg, and she looked down to see Lily staring up at her, her lip trembling.

"He's training, baby. Do you want to see?"

Lily nodded so Jade lifted her into her lap just as Sentu's tail lashed viciously across Inzen's cheek. She winced, sure that Lily would get upset but her daughter only settled back against her, her thumb in her mouth, watching sleepily.

This was the first time Lily had let her hold her, and the warm little weight in her arms made her heart ache. She lowered her head to brush it across her daughter's soft curls and breathe in her sweet, innocent fragrance. How much she had missed that scent. Together they watched Inzen, and she hoped that maybe she'd finally managed to reach her daughter.

That hope had faded later that night. They had eaten dinner with Cassie and her daughter again. Jade watched with interest as the other woman turned first pink, then white when Inzen announced that Sentu was coming to dinner. Apparently, Sentu's attraction wasn't completely one-sided.

Unfortunately, Lily wore herself out playing with Angel, and by the time they returned home, she was a cranky mess. Any hope of being alone with Inzen faded as he carried a crying Lily to what should have been their bedroom, throwing an apologetic glance at her over his shoulder.

She had waited for a little while but he hadn't reappeared. With a disgusted huff, she retired to the small bed in Lily's room once again.

This morning everything had been back to the unsatisfactory normal with Lily once more focused on Inzen. She couldn't begrudge her daughter's obvious happiness as they played in the garden, but she wished she could be part of it.

The Trevelorian version of a telephone rang and she went to answer it, finding Abby's smiling face on the other end.

"What's wrong?" the other woman immediately demanded.

"Is it that obvious?"

"You look like the world's coming to an end."

"I'm sorry. This mating business isn't working out very well."

"Why not?"

Abby's expression was curious but also sympathetic, and Jade found herself spilling her troubles in Abby's ear.

"And he won't even sleep with me!" she concluded and heard a startled breath. When she peeked hesitantly over her shoulder, Inzen was standing there, his eyes as hungry as they had been on the ship. He took one step towards her, and they both heard Lily call from the garden.

"Dada!"

He stopped dead, his tail flicking towards her even as his head turned to check on Lily.

"Go on," she said ruefully when he looked back at her.

"Very well. But we will discuss sleeping arrangements in greater detail tonight."

His eyes promised enough to make her body respond, even as she shook her head and turned back to find Abby still watching her, her face wreathed in smiles.

"Oh, believe me, I understand that. I can't tell you how many times Hrebec and I have been interrupted."

"Interrupted suggests that you got started to begin with."

"True. Do you want my advice?" Before Jade had a chance to answer, Abby waved her hand. "Never mind. I'm going to give it to you anyway."

Jade laughed. "I was going to say yes."

"First of all, Cassie." Abby sighed. "She had a really hard time back on Earth, in and out of foster homes—all of them bad from what I can tell. The people who were supposed to protect her didn't. I think Inzen is the first decent male she's ever known and she's jealous. Oh, not in a romantic way, but because he cares for her and she thinks she's going to be left out just like she was left out so many times before."

"He would never do that, and I would never ask him to."

"I know, but it's going to take her a while to understand that. I know it's hard but be patient with her. She'll come around—she's a smart girl and has a good heart underneath that cynical shell." Abby smiled. "And TeShawna will come with her. From what she's said to me, I suspect that she actually likes you already but isn't about to betray her friend by letting you know."

"It helps to know that she doesn't hate me too."

"She doesn't." Abby tapped her chin thoughtfully. "Now about Lily. You have to remember that she's, what, fifteen months old? That means she's discovering the power of saying no. You and Inzen need to work together and make sure you agree on what you let her get away with."

"I already know the answer to that one," she said gloomily. "He'll let her have whatever she wants."

"I understand, believe me. The Cire value children so much that they want them to have everything. I'm sure it's worse for Inzen because of the fact that he's already lost a child. But he's an intelligent male. He came to see me the day we found out about you because he knew that he was being overprotective. I'm sure he understands that she needs boundaries as well as love. Talk to him."

"All right." She knew Abby was right and realized that to a certain extent, she was as bad as her mate. She had let Lily dictate their lives because she couldn't stand to see her daughter upset.

Abby's eyes twinkled. "That being said, a little bribery can go a long way. Do you know how to make cookies?"

Jade laughed. She and Abby talked a little while longer and then, after they hung up, started making plans.

CHAPTER SEVENTEEN

All through dinner, Inzen found himself watching Jade. She seemed happier this afternoon, and he was grateful that talking to Abby seemed to have helped. The last few days had been difficult. Lily was unusually clinging and demanding, but he found it hard to say no to her after having left her. The first night she demanded to sleep with him, he had expected Jade to object. Instead, she simply left him and went to Lily's room. Was that what she wanted? Uncertain about her desires, he had let the situation remain despite his frustration.

At the training school, he had thought she was indicating interest, but last night when he finally got Lily settled and returned to the living area, Jade was no longer there and he decided she must have changed her mind. Hearing her complain to Abby about the arrangements had been a huge relief. Perhaps she really did want to be with him as much as he wanted to be with her.

After supper, Jade announced that she was going to make cookies. Lily instantly abandoned him and climbed back in her highchair so she could help. An hour later, she was sticky and smiling. Not once had she called for him, and he had been content to watch his two girls as they worked together.

When Jade would only allow her to eat one of the rather misshapen cookies, Lily started to pout. He opened his mouth to argue that one more wouldn't hurt but caught Jade's glare in time and hardened his heart.

"Not tonight, little one. Time for your bath. You have more cookie on your face than you have in your tummy."

"I'll take care of her bath tonight," Jade said, plucking Lily out of his arms. "Why don't we let Dada clean up the kitchen so we can make more cookies tomorrow?"

He could tell that Lily had been about to protest, but at Jade's words, she nodded.

"Dada clean."

Cleaning the kitchen was not as satisfying as watching his daughter play in the tub but he was relieved to hear her laughing and splashing despite his absence. When she emerged, clean and sweet-smelling in her little nightgown, she crawled up on his lap while Jade read her a bedtime story. Her eyes were drooping when the story finished.

"I think she's ready for her own bed tonight," Jade said softly as he picked Lily up to carry her to bed.

The thought of being alone with his mate made his shaft stiffen and he didn't object. As he started to put Lily down, her eyes opened.

"Sleep wif Dada."

"Not tonight, little one. You snuggle up with Bobo and I'll tell you another story."

Her scowl was interrupted by a big yawn, and to his immense relief, she put her arm around her stuffed animal, her thumb in her mouth, and closed her eyes again. By the time he finished the second story, she was asleep.

When he returned to the living room, Jade was waiting

for him. She had taken advantage of his absence to take a shower herself and she was wrapped in a simple green robe that revealed her delicate collarbone and her curvy golden calves. The thin fabric made it obvious she was naked beneath it, and he almost swayed as all the blood in his body rushed to his cock. Was she ready to become his mate in truth?

"You look very becoming, my letari."

"Not much of a letari right now, I'm afraid. You have neglected my training."

"You wish to train now?" It was not what he had in mind, but he would not turn down the opportunity to have her body against his.

"No, Inzen." Green fire sparkled in her eyes as she glanced slowly down his body. "But perhaps tomorrow. Tonight, we need to talk."

"Hrebec says it is not a good sign when a human female says those words."

She laughed and moved over to sit on the couch, patting the space beside her invitingly. "He may be right, but I still think we need to talk about Lily. And about us."

He sat next to her, unable to prevent his tail from curving around her waist. To his relief, she didn't object but nestled closer. A sense of rightness settled over him as his lungs filled with her sweet, spicy scent. This was where she belonged.

"What do you wish to say to me, my mate?"

"If we are to be truly mates—" she started, and his heart skipped a beat. *If?*

"—then we need to work together on everything."

"You wish me to work in the shop as well? I would be happy to do so although I know very little about female clothing."

She laughed again. "No, that's not what I had in mind. But

we need to work together to establish boundaries for Lily. I know you love her but that doesn't mean that she is in charge."

Guilt swept over him. "You are correct. I regretted leaving her, and I have not behaved as a father should. It is always difficult for me to discipline her."

"I understand but I can't always be the one to say no. I know she's having a hard time adjusting to me, but she'll never accept me if you're always between us."

"That was never my intention," he said, horrified.

"I know it wasn't." She patted his tail and he groaned. "Oops. Sometimes I forget that it's more than a friendly gesture."

"It feels as if you're stroking my cock."

Her eyes widened and she started to sway towards him, but then she pulled back, tilting her head to study his face.

"I think we should set up a schedule and alternate what we do with her so that sometimes I feed her and sometimes you do. Sometimes I give her a bath and sometimes you do."

"That sounds very reasonable."

"And if she cries and protests, we both tell her no."

He hated even the thought of tears in his daughter's big brown eyes, but Jade was correct. The child needed boundaries. He nodded, and she smiled at him with the most warmth he had seen since before his confession on the ship.

"And she sleeps in her own bed at night so that I can share yours."

He didn't even take the time to agree. He simply swept her up in his arms and carried her towards the bedroom.

Reluctantly putting her down, he turned to close the doors behind them. When he turned back, she was standing by the open door to his small garden, her clothing gone and her golden body glowing in the soft light of the garden lanterns.

"You are so beautiful."

"You make me feel beautiful." A smile played on her lips. "But you are wearing far too many clothes."

He reached for his tunic, but she shook her head. "Let me do that. Shouldn't a good mate help you undress?"

"It is a male's privilege to tend to his mate. It is not a common practice—"

Her hands slid beneath his shirt and he lost the ability to speak. Her tiny nails trailed across his skin, leaving a line of fire behind. Tugging the garment up his stomach in small increments, she kissed each inch of skin she revealed. She wasn't tall enough to pull it off completely, so he yanked it impatiently over his head.

"Mmm. That's much better." She leaned in and licked a soft pink tongue across his nipple, sending a spike of electricity to his aching cock. He reached for his pants to free himself, but she pushed his hands away. "Not yet. I'm enjoying myself."

How could he deny anything which gave his mate pleasure? He fisted his hands at his sides in order to avoid taking charge. His tail was not so restrained. It kept sneaking around to tug at one of her taut little peaks or test the slippery heat between her legs.

Shaking her head, she smiled up at him. "You have a very naughty tail."

"You are unbearably tempting."

"Hmm. I rather like the sound of that."

Her kisses resumed, skating along his waistband as she gradually pushed his pants down. They caught on his erection and she finally, finally freed his aching cock, laughing when the heavy length sprang free, liquid already pearling on his tip.

"Someone's happy to see me," she murmured. He lost all ability to think when she swiped her soft little tongue across him.

"My letari!"

She sank to her knees, gripping his cock in her small hand, and licked him again. "Is something wrong?"

"It is forbidden."

"What is? This?" Another longer lick, and he shivered. "Or this?" She took him into the heated depths of her mouth and sucked gently. The room swayed.

"Or is there something else I shouldn't do?" Her eyes were wide and innocent as she looked up at him, but he could see the teasing light sparkling there. Fuck if he could resist her.

"You definitely should not put your mouth on me again."

"Like this?"

Her lips closed around him once more and she took him deeper. He buried his hand in the dark, silky strands of her hair and groaned.

"Definitely not like that. You should not lick my cock either."

She let him slip out of her mouth, then slowly swirled her tongue around him, from his tip down to his throbbing base, where she enclosed his sack in the wondrous heat of her mouth.

"I suppose I shouldn't have done that either."

His control was at an end. "Take me in your mouth again."

She didn't hesitate, closing her mouth around him once more, sinking deeper on his shaft until her mouth met her hand. She started to pull back and his hand fisted involuntarily in her hair, but she only withdrew slightly before dipping down again. Over and over, slow sucking withdrawals were followed by rapid plunges until he could control himself no longer and exploded in a long shuddering wave. She still didn't pull back but drank eagerly until the final drop escaped, giving him a last lingering kiss as she sank back on her knees.

"You taste so good." She licked her lips and smiled up at him. "Too bad it's forbidden. I wouldn't mind doing it again."

"You will," he promised. To hell with rules that only

applied on a dying planet. What happened between mates was no one else's business, and if she enjoyed taking him into her mouth, he would let her do so whenever she wanted. "But now, it's my turn."

Before she could say anything, he scooped her up and carried her to the bed, dropping to his knees in front of her and parting her legs. Her delicate folds were already flushed and swollen, evidence that she had enjoyed their encounter as much as he had. He dragged his tongue across the damp flesh, determined to gather every drop of her delicious essence. She shuddered and clutched his head, awakening the sensitive nerves along his ridges and his cock throbbed, once again hard and ready, but he was determined to bring her as much pleasure as she had given him.

He brought her to climax three times, each time drinking eagerly of her sweet liquid, before he finally gave in and allowed his cock to sink into her. Unable to resist the feel of her hot, silken cunt after the long denial, his hips thrust helplessly, the base of his cock already swelling to lock them together as a second heated wave consumed him. His tail flicked across her pleasure receptacle, and he felt her quiver around him once again as he collapsed to the bed, holding her close as he sighed with contentment.

She was back in his arms, and all was right with the world.

CHAPTER EIGHTEEN

Jade yawned as she walked into Cassie's shop the next morning. Inzen had kept her up half the night—not that she was complaining—and would have continued his activities this morning if Lily hadn't called out for him. But instead of just abandoning her, he had brought Lily back to bed and the three of them had snuggled together. Lily hadn't complained once, and a budding optimism about her relationship with her daughter sent her off to work with a smile on her face.

Unfortunately, that smile dimmed as soon as she caught sight of Cassie. Something was obviously wrong. Dark circles stained the pale skin under Cassie's eyes, and the young woman looked exhausted. For once, her daughter Angel wasn't present.

"Is everything all right?" she asked softly.

"I don't know," Cassie snapped. "Have you been extending any more unwelcome dinner invitations?"

"I'm sorry. I didn't know you didn't want Sentu to come—"

"Of course you don't know what I want!" The other

woman stopped abruptly and rubbed her eyes. "Just go clean out the stockroom."

"I did that yesterday. Maybe I can help out with the customers today?"

"What customers?" Cassie flung her arm out towards the front window, and they both watched as two Trevelorian women glanced casually in the window and kept going.

Jade bit her lip before she provided what she was sure would be unwanted advice and started straightening the shelves. One side of the store was stacked with a variety of fabrics, many of them dyed with the amazing Trevelorian dyes to create shimmering, iridescent effects in bright jewel tones. The other side held some tasteful displays of premade clothing and a comfortable seating area for clients.

As the morning wore on, only one customer entered and Cassie's mood grew even darker. After they both watched a well-dressed matron pass by without a second look, Jade had had enough.

"Look, I know you don't want to hear from me, but I do have a lot of experience with selling clothes."

Cassie snorted. "On a strange planet populated by bird aliens? What good is your experience here?"

She thought back to the market on Driguera, not to mention what she had seen here on Trevelor.

"Retail is retail," she said firmly. "You're not getting any customers because your windows are too cluttered and your shop looks like every other shop."

"I was doing just fine until you came along."

"Really? Business just died off in the past few days?"

Cassie's glare turned even fiercer, but Jade saw the betraying color high on her cheekbones.

"It's been going down over the past couple of months," the other woman finally admitted.

"My guess is that when you opened up, the shop was something new so people were interested—"

"And now they're not?"

"It's not that they're not still interested. You have a group of regular customers, right?"

Cassie nodded.

"The problem is that you need to recreate that same excitement that was there when you opened."

"But I'm not new anymore."

"No, but you're still unique." Jade walked to the front of the store and pointed at the store window. "You're not showing how special your clothes are with a window that looks like every other window on the street."

"That's what the Trevelorians want to see."

"Maybe—from other Trevelorians. You should take advantage of the fact that you're different."

"What do you mean?"

"Get rid of all the clutter. Put no more than three outfits in the window and use a plain backdrop to set them off. Not all of them should be designed for Trevelorians. This town has lots of different species and seeing a variety of designs would let them know what you can do." Cassie was still scowling so Jade softened her tone. "You're very talented, Cassie. You just need to let people know that you have more to offer than the same outfits that anyone else could make."

"What makes you such an expert anyway?"

"This is what I did back on Earth."

Cassie scoffed. "Design shop windows?"

"Yes. And sewed and ran a cash register and acted as a buyer and did marketing and worked in our e-commerce division." A reminiscent smile crossed her face. "My grandmother believed that I should know every part of the business."

"And what was the business?"

"We have—had—a line of clothing stores. Forever a Lady was the most popular brand."

Cassie's mouth dropped open but before she could say anything, Inzen appeared at the back of the store with Lily in her stroller. Jade's lips curved into a happy smile at the sight of her family—Inzen's heated gaze reminding her of their night together and Lily waving cheerfully instead of scowling.

"Greetings, my letari," he said, running his eyes over her with equal appreciation. "I thought perhaps we could walk to the market and pick up some lunch at the stalls."

"That sounds wonderful." She shot a quick look at Cassie, who was still looking stunned. "Is it all right if I leave now?"

"Yeah, okay."

Jade could feel the other woman staring after her as they left.

"Is there something wrong?" Inzen asked.

"I hope not."

Revealing her past had been somewhat of a gamble. There was a good chance that Cassie would reject her even more now that she knew that she was the former owner of the popular clothing stores, but Jade hoped that she would at least think about listening to her instead. She had been quite sincere when she said that the girl had talent; she just needed to showcase it.

Inzen's tail wrapped around her waist and she leaned into him as they wandered down the street, away from the permanent stores into the stalls of the open market.

Bright colors surrounded them. Everything from the buildings to the colorful canopies over the stalls was decorated in brilliant colors that should have clashed but instead mingled into a cheerful whole beneath the turquoise sky. The Trevelorians were equally colorful with their variegated crests and brilliant outfits, but as she had mentioned to Cassie, a wide variety of other races were present as well.

They walked slowly around the edge of the market, stopping to pick up skewers of an unidentified but tasty meat and a small basket of something resembling fried potatoes. As they sat under the shade of one of the giant grass trees and fed Lily, Jade was filled with a vast contentment. Her daughter had actually agreed to sit on her knee and be fed, Inzen's tail was still firmly around her waist, and she was finally beginning to feel at home on this beautiful, interesting planet. She sighed happily.

"Are you well, my mate?" Inzen asked immediately.

"Very well. I have my daughter and I have you." She reached up and cupped his face, and his black gaze intensified.

"And do I have you?"

Before she could answer, Lily put a sticky hand on her cheek, mimicking her gesture.

"Cookie, Mama," she demanded.

Jade's eyes filled with tears. It was the first time that Lily had called her mama.

"I'm not sure that they sell them here, baby. Why don't we go back to the house and make some new ones? After your nap," she added as Lily yawned and snuggled against her.

"Do you want to put her back in her stroller?" Inzen asked.

"No." She didn't want to give up the warm little body nestled in her arms.

The three of them headed back to their house, stopping to look in the shop windows surrounding the market. Jade was delighted to find one that appeared to be a real estate broker with images of various properties on display.

"I always liked looking at houses," she told Inzen as he stopped to let her look.

"Do you wish to move? We do not have to share the property."

She considered the idea, then shook her head. Even if they had gotten off to a rocky start, she liked knowing that there were other human women nearby, and it would be good for Lily to have friends her own age as well. She still held out hope that she and Cassie would eventually be able to bond over their shared interest in clothing.

Inzen looked relieved at her decision.

"You don't want to leave, do you?" she asked.

"I do not. You know that I think of Cassie as a daughter. And I also like the fact that there is another mated Cire warrior present to watch over all of you when I am not there."

"Then why did you offer?"

"Because your happiness is most important to me, Jade. I—" Someone bumped into him and he gave a frustrated look around at the crowded surroundings. "We will talk more about this later."

Her pulse raced. Had he been about to tell her that he loved her? She already knew how much she cared for him and the words that almost escaped her the previous night, but everything was still so new. Keeping her face composed, she turned back to the window.

"I like this one, but why is it on stilts?"

"I believe that area floods in the rainy season." Inzen accepted the change of subject, and they laughed at a few of the more outrageous images, before he stilled, looking over her shoulder.

"I see someone I need to speak with. Will you wait for me here?"

"Sure, that's fine. Will you be long?"

"Just a few minutes. But do not leave here," he ordered.

He bent down and kissed her, his tail stroking her cheek before he strode off. Shaking her head at his bossy ways, she turned back to the window.

When the few minutes stretched to ten or more, she started

getting restless. Lily was asleep against her shoulder and she put her back in the stroller, shaking out her arm. The toddler weighed more than she had expected. Once Lily was buckled in, she turned to look for Inzen. People dodged in and out, carrying baskets and pushing small hand carts, while the colorful butterfly-like creatures that were the Trevelorian equivalent of birds swooped and danced overhead. At last, she spotted him on the far side of the market, his broad shoulders and gleaming green skin obvious even from a distance. Should she join him? He had seemed very firm about her remaining where she was.

As she debated, he stepped to one side and she saw who he was talking to. It was one of the furry aliens from the auction. A bead of cold sweat trickled down her back. He looked so much like the one who had tried to buy her.

It's a different species, she reminded herself. You don't know them well enough to pick out one in particular.

But then he raised his hand towards Inzen and she saw the gleam of metal around his wrist. Even from this distance, the red-tipped spikes were unmistakable. Her heart beat so rapidly that her chest ached. *Lord Gokan*. Why was he here? And more importantly, what was he doing with Inzen?

The alien pulled out a small bag and tipped it into Inzen's outstretched palm. Jewels cascaded from the bag, the light catching on their multitude of facets. Inzen's hand closed around them, and she realized that Gokan was paying him. But for what?

A moment later, the male waved his hands in the air, sketching out the curves of a woman's body as he laughed. He was too far away for her to hear, but she remembered the sound of his laughter all too well—and she remembered what he had said.

He would find her.

The memory of his hands around her neck cut off her breathing. She had to escape. Now.

Inzen tried to hide his disgust as the Ruijin male chatted amiably about his journey to Trevelor. The Ruijin were also a warrior race, but they valued brutality more than discipline and he had little respect for them. However, he did trust their ability to protect his purchase. When his jeweler had suggested that this male—Gokan—bring his purchase, he hadn't hesitated. Now, he was beginning to regret the decision.

"You brought them?" he asked impatiently as the male continued to ramble on.

"Of course I did. I had intended to make a trip to Trevelor anyway so when I heard that someone was looking for a courier, the timing was perfect."

Gokan started to slap Inzen on the back and his tail automatically intercepted the movement, clamping down on the male's wrist.

"No need for that. I was just being friendly." The male grinned, showing a mouthful of fangs, but Inzen could read the irritation in his eyes.

"I am anxious to conclude our business."

"Of course. Here they are."

The Ruijin opened his pouch and poured the gemstones into Inzen's hand. Perfect. He was especially delighted with the stones that matched Jade's eyes. Trevelor was a fine planet, but they did not possess any naturally occurring crystals, let alone ones worthy of his mate. He had arranged to purchase these from a jeweler on Driguera instead.

"May I ask why you wanted the jewels?"

"It is for a mating bracelet," he said briefly. Gokan threw back his head and laughed.

"Ah, a female." He made the shape of the female body in the air between them. "In these troubled times, you are lucky to possess one." He bared his fangs. "I thought I had found one, but she escaped my grasp. That's why I'm here."

Inzen frowned at him, not liking the other male's phrasing. "You are aware that it is a crime to pursue an unwilling female on Trevelor?"

The fake smile reappeared. "Of course. It's just natural female hesitation. They all need a little... persuasion, you know."

His tail quivered as a chill ran down his spine. He nodded curtly, already deciding that he would notify the authorities as soon as they parted.

"I must return to my family."

"Of course. With so few Cire females, you can't keep one waiting, eh?"

He started to slap Inzen's back again then drew back his hand in time. Inzen made no attempt to correct his assumptions about his mate but nodded again and went to find his mate and his daughter.

But when he returned to the property office, they were gone.

CHAPTER NINETEEN

Hands shaking, Jade ducked inside the small property office, trying to make sense of what she had seen. Why was Inzen accepting all of those jewels from the alien who had tried to purchase her? Her pulse raced as she remembered being at the male's mercy.

She had to get away from here. Now.

"May I help you, Mistress?" The Trevelorian female seated behind the desk studied her curiously, her beak-like nose twitching.

"I..." She tried to think coherently and found herself staring at one of the displays. "Are any of these available for rent? For just a short time?"

"I'm afraid not, Mistress. Our holiday rentals are over for the season. Our other properties are for sale only—wait a minute. I do have one property." The female eyed her doubtfully. "But it is very remote and only available for another week."

"That would be perfect. I'll take it." She winced, still not used to having so little money of her own. "I mean, how much is it?"

From the nominal sum mentioned, she suspected that the property was not only remote but primitive, but she didn't care. She pulled out the handful of credits that Inzen had insisted on advancing her against her salary and counted them, but it wasn't enough. Knowing her grandmother would want her to choose Lily's safety first, she took a deep breath and pulled off her jade ring.

"Would this be acceptable?"

"More than acceptable." The female shook her head. "The stone is quite rare. The ring is worth far more than the rental charge, and I don't have sufficient funds to pay you the difference."

"Do you have enough to allow me to rent a flyer?"

Opening her desk drawer, the agent nodded. "I do, but it is still not what you are entitled to receive."

"I don't care about that right now." The need to flee was searing through her veins. "Can you give me directions and tell me where to rent a flyer?"

"I can do better than that. My brother is in the rental business. I'll call him for you so he'll have it ready."

"Thank you so much—?"

"I am B'gento."

B'gento reached for her communication device but hesitated as Jade cast a nervous glance over her shoulder. She expected to see Gokan, looming in the doorway at any moment.

"Is something wrong?"

"I don't know. I just need some time to think." She looked at the other female's concerned face. "If a male—any male—comes looking for me, can you not tell him about this?"

"My dear, if someone is threatening you, we should go to the authorities."

The authorities? After the past year, her trust in the efficacy of the police had been shaken—they wanted to question rather than act.

"I just need to get away. Please." All those months of training, and now all she could think about was running. Her heart thudded against her ribs.

B'gento studied her a moment longer, then nodded, her orange feathers fluttering.

A few minutes later, Jade was on her way. Thankfully, Lily was still asleep in her stroller. She suspected that she was going to have a very unhappy little girl on her hands when she woke up and realized that her Dada was not there, but she needed time to think and there was no way she was leaving her daughter behind.

Lily was still asleep when Jade reached the rental depot. B'gento's brother must have been on the lookout for her because he opened the door as soon as she appeared and beckoned her inside, closing and locking the door behind her.

"I am B'hira. My sister says that you are in trouble."

"I really don't know if I am or not." Her mind was still in turmoil, struggling to explain why Gokan would have been handing all those jewels to Inzen. She straightened her shoulders. "But I don't want to take the chance. I have to get away from here so I can think safely."

Unlike the Trevelorian females, the males had multicolored crests. In addition to the orange his sister displayed, his crest also included shades of red and gold, and he flared it now in an impressive display as he frowned.

"You do not need to run. We Trevelorians would never permit a female and her child to be harmed. I would defend you myself."

Despite the full array of plumage, B'hira was only a little taller than Jade and she couldn't imagine that his thin legs or fragile feathered arms would in any way prevent Gokan if he came after her, but she was touched by his offer.

"Thank you, B'hira. I really appreciate that, but right now I just need to get away. B'gento said you could rent me a flyer to travel to the summer house?"

He sighed and nodded. "If that is the path you wish to take."

Leading her out of the small office and into a garage space holding a number of flyers, he escorted her to a small, neat vehicle in a soft shade of pink. It was neither as large nor as luxurious as Inzen's, but all that mattered was that it would get her out of here.

B'hira opened the door and showed her the simple controls. "I have already programmed it to take you directly to the summer house you rented. The map address is actually some distance from the house." He pointed to a basket resting on the floor. "She also asked me to put together a few supplies for you. It isn't much, but it will last a day or two."

Why was she always surprised by the kindness of strangers? She swallowed the lump in her throat and smiled at him.

"Thank you so much, and please thank B'gento for me. How much do I owe you?"

She fumbled for the credits that B'gento had given her in exchange for the ring, but he shook his head.

"Don't worry about it. My sister said that you gave her far too much for the rental, more than enough to cover the flyer as well. You hold on to your credits in case you need them."

The Trevelorians didn't shake hands but she bowed deeply in an attempt to convey her appreciation.

"Thank you again. I'll return the flyer as soon as I know what I'm going to do."

"There's no rush. We're heading into the rainy season and

there's always less demand at this time of year." He smiled down at Lily. "You just take care of yourself and your little one."

She returned his smile and bent down to pick up her daughter. Unfortunately, the movement disturbed Lily and her eyes opened. She gave Jade a sleepy smile, then looked past her, frowning at B'hira.

"Where Dada?"

"He's not here right now, baby. We're going to go for a ride." Lily's lip trembled and she clutched Bobo. "In this pretty pink flyer," Jade added hastily.

"Pink?" Lily tilted her head as she studied the vehicle, and then to Jade's relief, she smiled and nodded. "Ride."

As they set out, Lily babbled happily to Bobo, sufficiently distracted not to ask for Inzen. By the time the excitement began to pall, she started yawning again and fell back asleep, leaving Jade to her thoughts.

The Trevelorian countryside flew by and under other circumstances, she would have admired it. Rather than heading for the rolling farmlands where Hrebec and Abby lived, the flight plan took them into a more heavily wooded area, interspersed with a network of rivers and streams. The water, a deep purplish blue, sparkled as it flowed between grassy, many-trunked trees in vivid shades of lime and gold.

But despite the beauty of her surroundings, all she could think about was the encounter between Inzen and Gokan. She tried desperately to think of some logical reason why the furry bastard would have been paying Inzen, but she couldn't come up with any connection between the two males—except her. Maybe once she was safe, she could find a way to contact Abby and ask her to investigate.

Clouds started to appear just as the vehicle indicated the end of their flight, echoing her increasingly despondent mood.

She caught a glimpse of a faint track leading across a grassy meadow, then down a wooded hillside. Between the trees, she spied the house she had rented perched on sticklike legs and nestled into a small clearing next to one of the many streams. At least from the outside, the bright blue walls and thatched roof looked as charming as they had in the picture.

The auto control signaled the need for landing, and she carefully guided the flyer down next to the summer house. Once again, Lily woke up when she lifted her out of the vehicle, but she was immediately distracted by her surroundings. She bounced over to the edge of the stream and started collecting the multicolored pebbles that seemed to be a common feature of the Trevelorian riverbanks. Jade let her play, relieved that she hadn't started demanding Inzen as soon as they landed.

Inspecting her surroundings, she took a deep breath, some of the tension from the hectic flight finally leaving. Even though the sky had clouded over, it didn't detract from the peaceful serenity of the woods and stream. She hadn't seen any sign of nearby residences, and the knowledge that no one knew where they were was a weight off of her shoulders.

"Why don't we go see what it looks like inside the house?" she suggested once Lily had gathered a handful of pebbles.

When Lily nodded, she scooped her up and carried her up the stairs to the front porch that ran along the front of the building. The key B'hira had provided stuck in the lock, and for a horrible moment, she thought they would be locked out, but it finally turned and the door opened.

The inside of the house was as rustic as the outside but equally charming in a primitive way. The corners of the hut were rounded, and the two back corners contained circular beds woven from the native grasses. A smile crossed her lips for the first time as she realized that they resembled colorful nests.

Everything in the single room was a little shabby, the original bright colors faded, but it didn't detract from its cozy feel. A rough table sat in front of the wide window to one side of the door. In front of the window on the other side were two oversized, comfortable-looking chairs, perfectly positioned to look out over the clearing and down to the stream. She had a sudden vision of sitting there with Inzen, Lily snuggled in one of their laps, and her throat closed over. She missed him so much already.

As if reading her thoughts, Lily looked up at her. "Dada?"

"No, baby. He's not coming. Yet," she added hastily when her daughter's bottom lip trembled. "Why don't we see what we have for dinner?"

"Cookie?" Lily asked hopefully.

"I don't know about that," she said with a laugh. The Trevelorians didn't seem to be big on sweets. "But let's see what we can find."

Fortunately, the basket included some grazen fruit and Lily munched happily on those while Jade put together a simple meal. The sky outside continued to darken, the sun dropping below the horizon in muted shades of purple rather than the usual bright display, and it was fully dark by the time they had finished eating. Small round lanterns hung from the rafters and they came on automatically as darkness fell, casting a warm golden light over the interior.

An old but spotlessly clean tub occupied the space between the two nest beds, with a tiny but functional bathroom area behind it. She ran a small amount of water into the tub, stripped off Lily's clothes, and placed her in the tub with a couple of rubber cups to play with. While Lily splashed merrily, Jade shook out her daughter's dirty clothes and realized that in her mad rush to leave Wiang, she hadn't thought about clothing for the two of them. There was one change of clothes in Lily's stroller—she had learned that lesson already—but that was it, and all she had was the clothes she was wearing. She eyed the colorful bedding thoughtfully. Even though she didn't have all of her supplies, she could probably manage something.

By the time Lily was ready to climb out of her bath, Jade had turned one of the pillowcases into a rudimentary nightgown and pulled it down over Lily's head. Her daughter grinned happily.

"New jammies!"

"That's right. And you look very pretty in them."

Lily nodded complacently. "Pretty girl."

"Yes, baby. You are a pretty girl. Now let's curl up in bed and I'll read—I'll tell you a story."

After a short-lived panic when Jade couldn't find Bobo for a few seconds, she gathered Lily against her while she told her the story of the white fox, the wondrous animal who rewarded a hunter for saving her life by giving him the ability to cure a deadly plague. She could almost hear her grandmother's voice telling her the same story when she was a child. By the time she finished, Lily was already half asleep.

"Good night, baby," she whispered as she kissed her cheek. "I love you."

"Lub Bobo." Lily held up her toy for a kiss as well.

"Yes, I love Bobo."

"Lub Mama." Lily smiled sleepily up at her, then pouted. "Lub Dada."

"I know, baby. I love him too."

Wait—what? She had said the words automatically but the truth of them settled over her. Of course she loved Inzen. His kindness, his intelligence, the way he loved Lily, even his overprotective streak... It didn't matter that he was an alien or that they hadn't really known each other that long.

"I love him too," she repeated, still stunned by the revelation. And with the realization came the certain knowledge that he would never, ever conspire with a male who had tried to buy her as a slave. He had never been anything other than protective and loving to both her and their daughter. What a fool she had been to suspect him, even for a minute.

Oh God, he must be panicking now. She already knew there was no phone in the primitive summer house—she had to go back to town. But then she remembered that darkness had already fallen. Could she find her way back in the dark? She walked over to the window and pulled aside the curtain. The wind had risen as night fell and enough moonlight made it through the heavy clouds for her to see the grassy fronds of the trees whipping wildly in the stiff breeze. Would it toss the light flyer around as easily? She shuddered and let the curtain drop. She would have to wait until daylight.

Now that she had decided to return, her own foolishness haunted her. If Gokan was indeed after her, isolating herself was the worst thing she could have done. What if he was already trailing her? What if he found her here with Lily? She would do anything he said, anything to protect her daughter.

However, that didn't mean she had to give up without a fight. She searched through the kitchen drawers, pulled out the biggest knife she could find, and placed it on the table in easy reach. It didn't look like much and she added a heavy frying pan to her small collection of weapons. Adrenaline pumped through her body, and she knew there was no chance of falling asleep. She began moving through the training exercises that Inzen practiced but she was too tense to do them properly. Despite that, focusing on her breathing eventually helped calm her racing nerves.

With a mental apology to B'gento, she took one of the extra sheets and began making another outfit for herself and one for Lily. She heartily missed her advanced sewing tools, but she did the best she could, even though she had a hard time concentrating. Every time one of the trees in the surrounding forest brushed against the hut, she jumped.

The wind dropped for a second and she thought she caught the hum of machinery, but it was too faint to be certain. Her heart began to pound sickeningly against her ribs as her mouth went dry. Had Gokan found her?

She strained her ears, but it was almost impossible to hear anything over the wind through the stalks. Was that a footstep?

With the knife in one hand and the frying pan in the other, she moved as silently as possible to take up position behind the door. Yes, she was sure that she heard a step creak, followed by one of the boards on the porch. She tightened her grip on her weapons, her hands damp with sweat, and waited.

The door flew open and she moved automatically, trying to slam the frying pan down on the intruder's head and aiming for his ribs with her knife. Instead, the frying pan flew out of her hand as it collided with a rock-hard shoulder, and a ruthless hand seized the wrist holding the knife. She started to struggle, and then a familiar spicy scent washed over her.

"Inzen?"

His beloved face looked down at her, dark eyes wide with concern, and she burst into tears.

CHAPTER TWENTY

Inzen started back across the marketplace, frowning when he realized that Jade and Lily were no longer where he had left them. He was sure he had told Jade to remain here in front of the property office. He scanned the nearby stalls, wondering if they had wandered off to pick up another treat, but there was no sign of them. His tail lashed anxiously.

Trevelor was a safe planet and the Trevelorian authorities kept a close watch on the marketplace, but it was his responsibility to protect his mate and child. He should never have left them. His desire to surprise Jade with the mating bracelet had led him to make a foolish decision. When another look around still did not reveal their whereabouts, he decided they must have gone home. Perhaps Lily had awoken from her nap and become restless. *That must be it.* Determined to get home quickly, he tore through the marketplace, dodging the increasing number of shoppers who had started to appear as the heat of the day began to fade.

"Jade! Lily!" As soon as he burst through the gate into the garden courtyard, he began calling for them. The thought crossed his mind that he might wake Lily from her nap but at this point, he didn't care. He had to find them.

Only a cool breeze wafted through the empty cottage. Jade and Lily were not there. The drumming of his heart increased as he raced into the shop.

"Have you seen Jade and Lily?" he demanded.

Cassie looked up from where she was assisting a customer and frowned at him. "Not since this morning. Has something happened?"

"I do not know. They were waiting for me in the marketplace and when I returned, they were no longer there."

"She probably just wandered off," Cassie muttered. "Probably never even occurred to her that you'd be worried."

"Jade is neither selfish nor foolish. This has to stop, Cassie. She is my mate and she is part of my life and that is never going to change. If you cannot accept that, then perhaps it would be best if we moved out."

Cassie's face paled and she put an apologetic hand on his arm. "Please don't do that. You're my family."

"I am," he agreed as he patted her hand. "But that family is larger now and I need you to understand that."

"I'll try. Honestly." Cassie frowned as she looked over his shoulder towards the cottage. "You didn't see them anywhere else in the marketplace?"

"I did not but the crowds were beginning to increase. Perhaps I missed them."

Cassie suddenly clutched the countertop. "You don't think the Vedeckians came looking for her, do you?"

The nightmarish scenario flashed through his brain, and if he had not been a Cire warrior, his knees would have buckled. He forced himself to think logically and shook his head.

"The port is on the watch for their ships. They would have

alerted Hrebec if one requested a landing. And I saw no sign of them."

Cassie's customer, an older Trevelorian female with a carefully coiffed crest of red and silver feathers, interrupted.

"These people you are looking for—are they human?"

"Yes," he said eagerly. "Have you seen them?"

"I've been here in the shop with dear Cassie for the past hour. But my husband—he's the Market Master, you know—said something to me this morning about human females and someone searching for them." She ran a finger along her beak-like nose. "Now what was it he said? It was after he complained about the lack of grazen marmalade and I was explaining to him that it was difficult to import. Really, you know, you would think that the Confederated Planets would do a better job of restoring trade. It's been twenty years since the Red Death disappeared and it's still difficult to get certain items. Why, if it weren't for Cassie, I don't know how I would ever find anything appropriate to wear. Thank goodness she can outfit me—"

"Yes, she is very talented," he hastily agreed. "But what did your husband say about human females and someone looking for them?"

The matron tapped her nose again and he had the sudden urge to wring her thin neck, but he clenched his fists and waited for her to continue.

"Oh, yes, that was it. He said that there was a Ruijin in town asking about one." She shuddered. "Nasty, hairy creatures. If one can't have feathers, then I much prefer the simplicity of scales."

A Ruijin? Could she be talking about the courier?

"Why was he asking? Did your husband tell you?"

"I'm not exactly sure because I was trying to explain to our maid—a dear girl, but not the best at social etiquette—how to properly serve a cup of tea while he was talking... Oh yes, that was it. He heard the Ruijin had lost one and was determined to recover her."

He stared at her in appalled horror.

"What is it, Inzen?" Cassie asked.

"I spoke to one in the marketplace today. He came from Driguera. That is where the Vedeckians tried to sell Jade."

"Did you tell him about her?"

"No, thank Granthar. He thought I had a Cire mate. I do not see how he could have gotten to her before I did, but what if he had an accomplice?" This time, he clutched the countertop as the world spun around him. He could not stand to lose his mate and his daughter a second time.

"Inzen! Inzen, dammit. Listen to me." Cassie tugged urgently on his arm. "The transmitter. The one you have in Bobo. Does Lily have him with her?"

He tried to gather his thoughts into some semblance of order. Had Lily been carrying the stuffed toy in the stroller? Yes, he was sure of it. He fumbled in his pocket for the tracking device, praising the gods that he still carried it. His hand shook as he flipped open the cover to study the display. The signal was faint but still within reach.

"I do not understand. She is moving into the country. If the Ruijin had taken her, would he not head for the port immediately? He must know that he would not be permitted to keep an unwilling female."

"What if Jade saw him?" Cassie asked. "And now she's on the run."

"Why would she not have come to me for protection?" His chest ached and he rubbed it as he tried to understand what had driven his mate to run from him.

"You said you were talking to him. Did she see you?"

Could she have seen them? He supposed it was possible and then he groaned. "If she did see us, she would have seen him give me the gemstones he brought with him from Driguera."

"And she might have thought he was trying to pay you off." Cassie nodded grimly. "It would have been the first thing I suspected."

"I have to go after her now. If she has run away, I need to find her before he does."

"What if he already has them?" Cassie's eyes were wide with horror.

"Then I will kill him and retrieve my family." He started for the door, then turned back to the matron who had been listening intently. "Alert your husband. This male is dangerous and he must be stopped."

"Oh, yes, of course. Now where would he be…"

Her speculations drifted away behind him as he raced out of the shop. When he reached the transport shed where they kept their vehicles, he remembered that Mekoi had taken his flyer for the day. All that remained was the small hovercycle he'd purchased for Cassie.

He hesitated for a moment, but the signal was getting weaker and further away. He didn't have time to search for alternate transportation. Getting to his family was all that mattered. With a muttered oath, he swung aboard and set off.

Although he kept an anxious eye on the transmitter, the first part of the trip went smoothly enough. He had the small engine pushed to maximum power and he managed to stay in range. He breathed a sigh of relief when the signal stopped moving away. He prayed that it was because Jade had reached her mysterious destination and he would catch up with her at last.

Hold on, letari. I am coming for you.

A few minutes later, clouds began to roll in, the normally bright Trevelorian sky growing unusually dark. He paid no attention at first, but then he realized that the cycle was slowing. He tried to increase his speed, but the machine grew ever more sluggish as the skies darkened and he remembered that it was primarily solar powered. With the increasing cloud cover, he was forced to depend on the small supplemental battery that provided only enough power for the lowest setting.

By the time he reached the location indicated by the transmitter, darkness had fallen. He stopped at the top of a slight rise and saw lights gleaming from the windows of one of the small Trevelorian summer houses below. The sound of water indicated the presence of a nearby stream, but he was too focused on the house to care.

Fighting back the impulse to storm inside, he climbed cautiously down the hill, listening for any sign of trouble. Nothing disturbed the peaceful night. Even the insects were unusually quiet. He crept up on the porch, wincing when the wood creaked beneath his feet.

One of the curtains was ajar and he peeped inside. The room looked empty and his heart sank, but then he caught a glimpse of a small body tucked in one of the wall beds. Lily! But where was Jade?

Anxiety overcame his caution and he couldn't wait any longer, throwing the door open and rushing inside. The minute he crossed the threshold, a heavy object came crashing down on his shoulder. He growled and whirled around, instinctively grabbing his assailant in a bone-crushing grasp and forcing him to his knees. But instead of looking down at the Ruijin's ugly face, he found himself looming over Jade, her face pale and her eyes frightened.

"Inzen?" she whispered, and then she burst into tears.

CHAPTER TWENTY-ONE

Was she so unhappy to see him? Inzen's chest ached as he carefully released her wrist and stepped back.

"Do not cry, my letari. I am not here to hurt you, just to protect you. I am sorry if my presence distresses you."

"Distresses me? I've never been so glad to see anyone in my life."

"You are glad I am here?"

"Of course I am. I'm so sorry I ran away. Can you ever forgive—"

Her babbled apologies ended as he brought his mouth down over hers, relief weakening his knees. She clung to him just as desperately and he could taste her tears in the kiss as he devoured her mouth.

"Thank Granthar you are all right," he muttered when he finally forced himself to raise his head.

"We both are, despite my stupidity. When I saw Gokan give you those jewels, I just panicked. I should have had more faith in you."

Gokan. His eyes closed in despair as he realized that his

theory that the Ruijin was the one who had tried to purchase her was correct.

"I wish you had," he agreed. "But I realize how it must have looked."

"Why did he give them to you? What was he paying you for?"

"He wasn't paying me at all. He simply served as a courier after I ordered them from a jeweler on Driguera."

"I don't understand. Why did you buy jewels?"

He sighed. "I wanted to make you a mating bracelet. It is an ancient Ciresian custom, not practiced for many generations, but it was a foolish idea, made more so by my wish to keep it secret. What matters is that your heart belongs to me, not that you wear any outward symbol of our union. I can only regret that my pride caused you any doubts. I hope you know that I would never let any harm come to you or to your daughter—"

"Our daughter," she corrected, and happiness filled him. "I realized that tonight. She belongs to both of us. Just as I realized that you would never let anyone hurt us."

Heart too full for words, he gathered her closer, his arms and tail enclosing her in his embrace as he let her sweet, spicy scent wash over him. She sighed happily and snuggled into him. Across the small room, he could see Lily tucked under a colorful sheet, her cheeks flushed with sleep.

He had his family back.

Gathering Jade up in his arms, he carried her to one of the chairs in front of the window and settled down with her on his lap. They sat in contented silence for a moment and then she looked up at him.

"How did you find us? Do you think Gokan could track us the same way?"

"The Ruijin? No, my letari. I found you because I have a transmitter in Bobo."

Her eyes widened. "You bugged a stuffed animal?"

"Bug? I would never allow her toy to be infested by insects."

"It's just an expression. A bug is a tracking device."

"I see. Yes, I implanted the device when I learned that keeping track of Bobo was critical to Lily's happiness. And my ability to sleep."

"Bobo does seem to be able to disappear. I had a hard time finding him earlier and there aren't exactly a lot of places to hide in here."

"Where did you find him?"

She shook her head. "Hiding behind the curtain. I could have sworn Lily had never been near there, but fortunately I found him before she panicked." Her gaze dropped and she ran a finger down his chest, igniting an arousal completely out of proportion for the casual gesture. "She missed you."

"And did you miss me also?"

"I did." She looked up at him, more tears shimmering in those crystal green eyes. "In my heart, I knew you would never betray me, but my head is still used to expecting the worst. Yet even with my doubts, I still wanted you to be here with us. Maybe we could stay here for a few days? And just have some family time?"

"That sounds wonderful, my letari, but unfortunately, I need to return to Wiang to oversee the search for Gokan. I want to make sure that he will not cause us any trouble."

Her eyes widened. "I thought you said he wouldn't be able to track us here?"

"I do not believe he can, but I am not prepared to take any chances. He should be arrested anyway for his attempt to purchase a slave."

A flash of lightning was followed by the loud crack of

thunder and she shivered. The sound of the rain on the roof increased to a constant drumming.

"At least I'm pretty sure that he won't be out looking for me tonight."

"It is an unpleasant night," he agreed. It would not have stopped him from hunting down his mate and child, but he suspected that the Ruijin would be far less determined. "But it is early for the rainy season to start. I anticipate that the weather will clear tomorrow. Instead of taking you and Lily back to Wiang with me, I thought perhaps I would take the two of you to visit Hrebec. That way, you will be safe while I deal with that bastard."

"You mean I'm going to lose you again so soon?" Her bottom lip pouted out in a gesture very similar to the one that Lily used but her expression was far from childish. She swiped a teasing finger along her lip, and he wanted to follow it with his tongue. "In that case, we better make the most of tonight."

"But Lily..." he protested half-heartedly, his stiff cock already aching.

"You know what a sound sleeper she is. We'll just have to be very, very, very quiet."

With each word, she rubbed herself against his erection. Unable to resist, he cupped a small perfect breast, her hardened nipple stabbing his hand. He stroked across the tempting nub and slowly shook his head.

"I do not know. It is very bright in here."

She had been arching into his hand but when he spoke, she pulled back and glared at him. His tail curved over her leg, and he rejoiced at the slippery heat that met his touch. Her expression softened as her legs parted for him.

"Are you teasing me?"

He circled the swollen pearl of her clit and she gasped.

"Does this count as teasing?"

"It does if you're going to leave me hanging."

"What would I hang you from?" he asked, his gaze flying to the rafters. A sudden vision of her slim golden body, arms stretched up to emphasize her slender curves, assaulted him. He would be free to kiss and caress every part of her in such a position. "I am most intrigued by the possibilities, but do you think this is an appropriate time?"

"Possibilities, hmm?" Her eyes darkened, and the sweet scent of her arousal intensified. "I'm not sure what you have in mind but I'm sure I would enjoy it. However, as you so rightly said, it's too bright in here."

"The light I can remedy." The control panel was conveniently located on the wall to the right of his chair, and he dimmed the lanterns to the softest possible glow. Her face was barely visible, but he could see her smiling.

"I didn't even know that was there. We would have slept with the lights on." She shivered and snuggled closer. "Although I don't think I would have minded. I was already jumpy enough. I mean, I was nervous," she added before he could ask.

"But you no longer wish to jump?"

"No, Inzen. As long as you're here, I know we're safe." She took a deep breath, her breasts rubbing pleasurably against his chest. "I know something else as well. I love you. I'm just sorry it took me so long to realize it."

Happiness exploded in his veins. She was truly his at last. The words he wanted to say would not come so instead he showed her. He worshipped her mouth and her breasts until she was writhing against him, her breath coming in rapid pants. But he wanted—*needed*—more. Rising to his feet, he carried her to the empty bed, stripping away both of their clothes, before he knelt over her. He grasped her small hips and brought her delicious cunt to his mouth, barely able to keep from moaning as her sweet taste filled his mouth. She gasped, surprisingly loud in the quiet room, and he brushed his tail against her mouth to remind her to keep quiet. To his shock, the hot wetness of her mouth closed around the sensitive tip as her hands seized his tail.

Once again, it took all of his self-control to avoid moaning. Each stroke of her hands and each lick of her tongue went straight to his aching cock, but he concentrated on the damp flushed folds against his mouth. More liquid heat met his tongue as she pushed impatiently against his face, her grasp tightening on his tail. He concentrated on her small pleasure receptacle, hot and hard against his mouth as he licked and sucked. He shifted his grip so that he could put first one finger, then another into the soaking heat of her channel. His thumb slid through her wetness then probed at the delicate star of her bottom hole. As he pushed gently but firmly inside, her entire body shuddered and her body clamped down on him, so tight he could barely move as she pulsed around him.

He could wait no longer. As soon as her grip loosened, he flipped her over on her hands and knees and came down over her, pushing a pillow towards her.

"Use that," he managed to say as the head of his cock found her soaking entrance. She grabbed the pillow and buried her head in it as he entered her in one long hard plunge. He heard her muffled scream of pleasure, felt her body convulse again, but he was too far gone to hesitate, stroking into her again and again, taking her, claiming her.

His mate. His love. His.

The base of his cock swelled, knotting them together as the explosion rose up through his body like a tidal wave, his seed leaving him in pulse after pulse of heated pleasure until he was limp and drained. Collapsing to the bed, he kept her snug against his body as he rolled to the side, trailing soft kisses across her shoulders.

"You did very well keeping quiet, my letari," he said after he got his breath back.

"Just as well you gave me the pillow." She giggled quietly and the vibrations sent a surge of pleasure straight to his cock. Her snug channel tightened around him as she shivered with pleasure. "Don't you ever get soft?"

"Not around you, my love. But my knot will go down."

Her breath caught as she looked at him over her shoulder, her eyes wide in the dim light. "Do you mean that?"

"Mean what? You know that the swelling will subside."

"Not that. I mean, do you love me?"

How could she have any doubt? He cursed their position since it wouldn't allow him to face her directly, but he curved his hand around her face.

"I think that I have loved you since the first moment when our eyes met in the medical bay, but I knew it for sure when you stopped that pickpocket and then insisted that we should let him go. Even if Lily had not been your daughter, I would have wished to make a family with you."

She turned her head and kissed his palm, the brush of her lips both sweet and sensual as she covered his hand with her own.

"And now we're really a family."

CHAPTER TWENTY-TWO

Jade woke up feeling warm and cozy. She could still hear the rain beating against the roof, and it was almost enough to make her want to snuggle down under the covers and go back to sleep. Except... Inzen was wrapped around her, his tail over her waist and his hand cupping her breast. His cock—his very erect cock—had worked its way between her thighs and she could feel it rubbing pleasurably against her clit as she shifted position. She moved again, hoping to increase the pressure, and Inzen growled into her ear.

"If you keep moving like that, my letari, I am going to assume that you are interested in morning bed sport."

She squeezed her legs together and they both groaned, then she smiled at him over her shoulder. He smiled back, his eyes heated but his face soft and loving.

"I might be interested," she whispered. "If you can persuade me..."

His eyes darkened, and he flipped her effortlessly on her back as he rose over her.

"Challenge accepted."

He bent his head to kiss her, that marvelous nubbed tongue leisurely exploring her mouth. She reached up to stroke his ridges and the kiss intensified. His tail plucked at an erect nipple and she arched against him.

"Have I persuaded you?" he murmured, and she laughed breathlessly.

"I might need a little more—"

"Dada!"

The demanding little cry echoed through the small cabin and he shook his head ruefully.

"It appears that we will have to wait."

"I don't mind. You're worth waiting for."

He bent his head to give her another kiss and…

"Mama!"

Her chest ached to hear her daughter calling for her at last. She started to sit up, but he gently pushed her back down.

"Wait here and I will bring her to you. The cabin is a little cool this morning. Let me see if I can find a heater."

Now that he mentioned it, she realized that the air was colder than it had been since she arrived on Trevelor. It was even more obvious after he climbed out of bed, taking his warmth with him. A minute later, he returned with Lily in his arms and tucked her and Bobo in bed with her. To her relief, Lily smiled happily and snuggled against her but when she looked up at Inzen, he was frowning.

"Is something wrong?"

"It appears that the rainy season is beginning early. It would be of no consequence if we were in town, but I have never experienced it in the countryside."

"Would it be different here?" She was a city girl herself.

"I do not know. Stay under the covers and keep warm."

Lily started to squirm restlessly, so Jade entertained her with a game of itsy-bitsy spider. It seemed appropriate under the circumstances. Before her daughter had a chance to get tired of the game, Inzen returned, his face grim.

"I am afraid we may have a problem," he said quietly as he handed both of them one of the breakfast bars that B'hira had provided.

Lily chewed happily, pretending to feed bites to Bobo, and Jade tried to ignore the crumbs she was scattering in the bed.

"What is it?"

"The stream is rising rapidly. Can you hear it?"

Now that he mentioned it, she could hear a soft roar underneath the constant beat of the rain. She shivered as she remembered how close the bank was to the cabin.

"Do you think it will wash away the cabin?"

He hesitated just a fraction too long before answering her. "I do not believe so, my letari. This building has been here for many years and it appears to be sturdy. But it was not designed to be inhabited during this season. There is no source of heat."

"We also don't have any food other than what was in the basket B'hira gave us. I guess we'd better get ready to go."

His tail lashed anxiously, and his face didn't lighten.

"Leaving may be difficult. The flyer is partially underwater."

"Oh no." She stared at him in dismay as she remembered bringing it to land in the open space in front of the cabin. If that area was already underwater...

"What about the hovercycle?"

"It is still safe because it is at the top of the hill, but I cannot take both of you at once. It is designed for Trevelorians and already struggles with my weight. There is also little room to carry three." His tail lashed again. "Perhaps I can instruct you on how to drive it and you can take Lily to safety."

"What about you? I'm not going to leave you here."

"The temperature does not bother me as much as it does the two of you. I can wait until the water drops."

"And how long will that take?"

He shrugged unhappily. "If the rainy season has truly started, the rains could last three or four days. Or perhaps a week. Once they stop, the water recedes rapidly."

"A week?" She frowned. Not only did she not want to be separated from him for that long, but there was also the problem of her unwanted pursuer. "What if Gokan comes after me?"

"I told you that I would send you to Hrebec. He will protect you." Despite the reassuring words, he didn't seem happy about the idea. "And perhaps I can walk out after you. I should be able to cover the distance in a day, perhaps two."

"That's ridiculous. I don't want you walking through the pouring rain." She looked down at Lily, who was now tugging off one of the pillowcases to make a dress for Bobo. "Can the hovercycle carry you and Lily?"

"Yes, but—"

"What about you and me?"

"Perhaps, but it would be very slow."

"As slow as walking?"

He shook his head. "What are you suggesting, my letari?"

"Cold, Mama," Lily said as she climbed back onto her lap with Bobo, and Jade automatically wrapped her arms around her.

The words almost caught in her throat, but she lifted her chin and continued. "Why don't you take Lily first? You can take her to Hrebec and Abby and then return for me."

She hated the thought of being separated from her daughter, of sending her out on a flimsy machine under these conditions, but she knew Inzen was right. They could not stay here.

"I do not want to leave you."

"I don't want you to either, but it makes sense. You can get Lily to safety and then come back for me. If it takes a little longer for us to get back, at least we'll be together and we'll know she's safe."

"You trust me to do this?"

"Yes." She didn't even hesitate. He had never been anything but honest, protective, and loving, and she trusted him completely.

"I do not like the idea of leaving you," he repeated.

"Like you said, there's no reason that anyone would know that I was here. No one else has a secret transmitter hidden on us, right?"

"No, my mate." He looked down at Lily, using her hands to walk the spider up the spout, and frowned. "I do not like to take her out in these conditions."

"It's only a little rain." As if in answer to her words, the drumming on the roof increased and she gave him a rueful smile. "Okay, a lot of rain. But we'll wrap her up well and you can tuck her against your chest. How long will it take to get to Hrebec?"

"An hour? Perhaps a little less."

"Then she'll be fine," she said firmly, doing her best to hide her own concern. She smiled down at her daughter. "Are you ready to go for a ride with Daddy, Lily?"

"Ride?"

"Yes, baby. On his cycle. It flies in the air and goes vroom, vroom."

"More like splutter, splutter," Inzen muttered, but he scooped Lily up and flew her around the room making *vroom, vroom* noises. She giggled happily, and Jade forced herself out of the warm bed to locate everything she could wrap around her daughter.

Inzen cut head and arm holes in the final two pillowcases

and they dropped them over her head, then wrapped her in towels. When he tucked Lily inside his tunic, she started to wiggle and protest, but Jade told her that they were playing kangaroo and Lily accepted it.

"Are you sure about this?" Inzen asked as they walked out onto the porch. From here she could see the muddy water swirling beneath the cabin, indistinguishable from the stream. Only the top of the pink flyer was still visible. The rain continued to beat down around them. Even the leaves of the grassy trees were bending towards the ground.

"I'm sure. Just be careful." She forced a smile. "If the conditions get worse, and you need to take longer, don't worry about me. I'll be fine."

"My brave letari." His tail circled around her waist and pulled her closer. "But there is nothing in this world or the next that will stop me from coming back for you."

He dropped a quick kiss on her lips and turned towards the stairs.

"Mama, come," Lily demanded, her lip trembling, when she realized that Jade wasn't following them.

"Not right now, baby. I'll catch up with you in a little while."

"Mama!" she wailed, and Jade saw Inzen hesitate. He cast a troubled look at her over his shoulder before he tightened his arms around Lily and descended the steps.

The water reached up to his thighs and her heart skipped a beat as he staggered, but then his tail rose, balancing him, and he hurried up the hill, Lily still protesting. With the wet leaves weighed down by the rain, she could watch them climb aboard the flimsy-looking hovercycle. It looked much too small for Inzen's big body, and she held her breath until it lifted into the air. He turned towards her and she forced herself to smile and lift a hand in salute. He raised his own hand and then the cycle flew slowly away, leaving her alone with nothing but the pounding of the rain and the rushing water.

Without her daughter or her mate, the small cabin seemed lonely and rather shabby. The remnants of her previous sewing efforts still littered the kitchen table and she picked them up with a sigh. Even if they were no longer necessary, at least it would give her something to do.

The rain continued in a steady downpour while she sewed but it lightened enough that she heard the soft thud of a footstep on the porch and spun around eagerly.

"That didn't take you long—"

Her words came to an abrupt halt. Instead of Inzen's big body, the Ruijin filled the doorway. He had found her.

CHAPTER TWENTY-THREE

"Did you expect me to linger? I told you that I would track you down, human." Gokan raised a shaggy brow. "I would have been here sooner if the Trevelorian navigation systems weren't so primitive. I had to walk in from the road."

A bead of cold sweat slid down her spine, but she kept her face calm and raised her chin. Thank God Lily was no longer here.

"I was not expecting you at all. I was expecting my mate."

"Your mate?" He threw back his head and laughed, revealing a disturbing number of gleaming white fangs. "One does not mate with those from a primitive planet. Although, they do have their uses."

His eyes slid over her with obvious lust and she had to hide a shudder of revulsion. She refused to give him the satisfaction of knowing how much he repelled her.

"Not everyone feels that way. I am mated and he will return shortly."

"Your mate? Is he one of these fragile little Trevelorians?"

He sneered as he strode casually into the room. "The last one I encountered fainted from no more than a single broken bone. I would have been most annoyed if it hadn't been for the fact that she was in the process of recording the rental of this property—to a human. That was all I needed to track you down."

"B'gento?" she whispered, her stomach rolling at the thought of this brutish alien putting his hand on the Trevelorian's delicate bones. "What did you do to her?"

"Not as much as I could have done. She should be grateful that I don't find feathers stimulating." He gripped the bulge between his legs suggestively as he leered at her. "Unlike all that naked flesh of yours. It will show every one of my marks."

"I didn't mate a Trevelorian," she said furiously. "I mated a Cire warrior. Inzen will destroy you."

"Inzen?" To her astonishment, he threw back his head and roared with laughter. "You must see the humor. I was the courier who brought him the gemstones he purchased. He mentioned that the stones were for a mating bracelet, but he never told me that it was for a human. How unfortunate that he will never get the chance to give it to you."

"Yes, he will. He'll come for me. You're no match for him," she sneered, and the amusement left his face.

"I am a Ruijin warrior in my prime. He could—perhaps—be a minor challenge but he would never defeat me. You would see for yourself if it weren't for the fact that we will be long gone before he returns."

"That doesn't matter. He'll never stop looking for me." The truth of that echoed with every beat of her heart, but she didn't want Inzen to suffer through the pain of searching for her. She eyed Gokan. He looked too bulky to be much of a swimmer and she swam twice a week. If she could just get past him, she'd take her chances with the river.

Feinting to the right, she ducked to the left instead, trying to reach the frying pan still sitting on the kitchen table. Unfortunately, the Ruijin intercepted her, tugging her up against his body, the spikes of his chest armor pressing painfully against her back as he ground his crotch into her ass. She struggled wildly but he was so much larger and stronger she had a hard time getting leverage. Even when she clawed at him, her nails couldn't penetrate his thick fur.

Remembering when she had trained with Inzen on the ship, she tried leaning into him instead. His grip relaxed just enough that she started to slip free. She had almost escaped his grasp when his hand clamped down on her wrist, yanking her back with painful pressure. Before she could renew her struggle, cold, hard metal encircled her neck. Shock kept her motionless as he stepped back, laughing.

"Do you remember that, human? I obtained it from Master Eiran. He was only too glad to hand it over after sponsoring that debacle of an auction." He shook his head in mock regret. "I only hope his successor is more successful."

Her stomach churned. She had no sympathy for the slave master, but Gokan's cheerful brutality nauseated her.

Outside the cabin, the rain had diminished a little, no longer drowning out all other sounds. Her heart started to beat faster as she thought she caught the faint hum of a flyer. Had Inzen returned already? She had to distract the Ruijin.

"You killed him?" she asked. "Do you cause damage everywhere you go?"

"Only when it's necessary." He flashed his fangs again. "Fortunately, it's often necessary."

She put her hand to the collar and glared at him. "I thought you said you didn't need this?"

"I don't. Once we return to my ship I have much more

entertaining ways to train you, but I don't have the time to fight you all the way back to Wiang, no matter how amusing it might be."

Even as she kept him talking, she listened, desperately hoping to hear the sound of someone approaching. Her heart raced as she heard a soft whisper of sound from the top of the hill. Had the flyer landed?

For once, her stoic mask must have failed her because the Ruijin's eyes sharpened and his ears flicked up. He crossed to her in a single step, just as she opened her mouth to scream out a warning. A huge furry paw clamped down across her face before she had a chance to call out.

"So the eager mate returns, does he?" he murmured in her ear as the disgusting odor of his fur surrounded her. "I almost hate to do this. It would give me immense pleasure to let you watch me defeat him, but I'm afraid you might get damaged in the process and I take better care of my toys than that."

He raised his right paw and she saw the control to the shock collar.

"Still, perhaps I will bring his head along as a reminder that it's impossible to defeat me." As he spoke, he pressed the button, and a fiery wave of pain spiraled out from the collar, traveling along every nerve as her body spasmed and she collapsed to the ground.

Her vision turned dark but only for an instant and she didn't lose consciousness. As the pain washed over her, she remembered that day on the ship when Kwaret had adjusted the collar to the lowest intensity.

Gokan didn't even bother to look in her direction, obviously assuming she was now unconscious. Instead, he moved into position behind the door, the same position she had taken the night before. If the pain throbbing through her body hadn't been so intense, she would have smiled. Despite his boasts about his skills, he still wasn't confident enough to face Inzen directly. But she couldn't let him take advantage of her mate, even though she could barely move.

Struggling to turn her head, she searched desperately for a weapon. Her body had fallen to the ground between the two big chairs and she spied a gleam of metal under the closest one. *The knife!* After Inzen had taken it away from her the previous night, he had dropped it to the floor, and it must have skidded underneath the chair. She tried to reach for it, but the aftereffects of the shock collar had caused her muscles to seize up. Sweat poured from her body as she gradually forced her arm to reach forward until her hand closed around the knife handle.

Water splashed, then the porch steps creaked. Inzen was here—she was out of time. Calling on every ounce of love and determination she possessed, she tightened her grip on the knife. As the door began to open, she threw herself at the Ruijin's leg with a hoarse cry. The blade slid into his flesh with sickening ease and he growled. He started to turn towards her and then Inzen was there.

Overcome by the effort, she fell back to her knees, her vision fading in and out as she caught brief glimpses of the battle raging between the two warriors, their bodies colliding with brutal violence. Finally, she heard a sharp crack, and then Inzen threw the Ruijin's body aside as he rushed over to her and lifted her into his arms.

"Jade! Are you all right?" His face blurred over her, her vision shrinking into a single dark spot, but she managed to smile.

"Love..." she whispered before the darkness took her.

. . .

Inzen's heart skipped a beat as Jade's eyes fluttered close. No! By Granthar, he couldn't be too late. He bent closer and felt the soft brush of her breath and then the beat of her heart, fast but steady. Relief overwhelmed him and he collapsed to the ground, still cradling her in his arms.

Thank Granthar he hadn't dallied with Hrebec. The trip to his former captain's home had been painfully wet and slow, and Lily had been miserable, despite his efforts to shield her. But she had proven to be her mother's daughter, handling the entire experience with determined bravery. When they finally made it to Hrebec's, his growing sense of urgency wouldn't allow him to rest. After sending a message to Cassie and making sure that Lily was once again safe and warm, he had demanded the loan of a flyer. Lily had started to protest his leaving, but when he told her that he was going to get her mama, she had let him go without any further argument.

The whole way back to the hut, he had been plagued by an increasing sense of doom but hadn't anticipated finding the Ruijin waiting for him. The smell of blood had been the only thing that had alerted him to his presence. That and the hoarse cry that he now recognized must have come from Jade's lips.

He scowled at the shock collar circling her delicate neck, her golden skin reddened along the edge of the device. What had that bastard done to her? He wanted to remove it, but he was loath to let her go, even for the length of time it would take to find the controls. Instead, he cradled her against his chest, rocking her back-and-forth as he murmured words of love to her unconscious body.

Water splashed outside, and he heard footsteps on the porch. Had the Ruijin been accompanied by more of his kind? Reluctantly, he lowered Jade to the ground and stepped in front of her. No one would ever hurt her again.

The door opened but instead of another Ruijin, Hrebec appeared.

"I heard there was trouble in town. A Trevelorian female was attacked, and I was concerned that it was related to your mate." His gaze traveled past Inzen to the body on the floor. "However, I see you have already taken care of the problem. Did he harm your mate?"

"I know that he shocked her, but she was conscious enough to stab him." Despite his concern, fierce pride filled him as he gathered her back in his arms. She was truly a warrior. "I want to remove the collar—can you check for the controls?"

Hrebec bent over the Ruijin's body for a moment, then handed him the device. Inzen had to fight back a snarl as the other male approached, even though he knew Hrebec would never harm Jade. She was unconscious and vulnerable and he hated having anyone close to her.

"Be easy, my friend," Hrebec said softly while Inzen removed the collar and threw it to one side. "She is safe in your arms and she will need you to be calm for her."

He sighed, forcing his protective instincts under control. "I know. She needs to be examined as soon as possible to make sure that she has suffered no lasting injury."

"I agree. Do you want to follow me back to the village? Or perhaps you would prefer to accompany me in my vehicle? It will be difficult to fly and hold her at the same time."

He didn't like the idea of being in an enclosed space with another male but neither did he want to be distracted from watching over her. "Very well."

As he started to stand, Jade's eyes fluttered open and she immediately focused on his face. "You're safe."

"Of course. You did not have to take a foolish chance in order to ensure my safety."

She frowned up at him. "Would you have let him ambush me?"

"Of course not. You are a very brave letari. But I do not wish you to try and protect me."

"We protect each other," she insisted, her eyes sparkling with their usual fire, and he gave a relieved laugh. She was back with him.

CHAPTER TWENTY-FOUR

Exhausted, Jade let Inzen carry her to Hrebec's flyer without protest. Even though the rain was still pouring down, he kept her cradled so close against his chest that she was barely wet when he sat down with her in his lap and she was grateful not to add being soaked to her other miseries. Her neck hurt, her throat hurt, and her entire body ached with the after-effects of the shock. *Shame Kwaret hadn't been able to turn it down a little more*, she thought wryly, then was immediately ashamed. If it hadn't been for the Vedeckian's assistance she would still be unconscious on the floor of the cabin—or perhaps being carried away by the Ruijin with Inzen dead or injured. She shuddered and Inzen immediately looked down at her, his face worried.

"Are you in pain, my letari?"

"No - well, yes, but it's nothing serious. Just aches and pains."

"We will have you examined as soon as we reach the village," he assured her.

"I don't think that's necessary -"

"It is necessary. I want to make sure you have come to no harm through my carelessness."

"What on earth are you talking about? You weren't careless."

His dark eyes were filled with guilt. "I left you alone to be attacked by that bastard."

"Inzen, you were taking our daughter to safety. I'm so thankful she wasn't there when he arrived." She lifted a shaky hand to touch his cheek. "And you came back to rescue me."

"I will always come for you, my love."

"I know. For me and for our daughter." She knew that Inzen would never have left their daughter unless she was safe, but she had to ask. "And Lily is all right? The trip wasn't too much for her?"

"She was as brave as her mother. Abby was giving her a hot bath and promised to make her something called hot choclot."

"Hot chocolate? Here? That sounds wonderful."

"Then you shall have some too," he promised.

"Abigail and my girls are most fond of it," Hrebec said from the front of the flyer. "Especially during the rainy season." He peered through the front window. "It started unusually early this year."

"So I gathered," she said dryly, remembering the water swirling around the summer house and the half-drowned flyer. She would have to find some way to pay B'hira for damage—*oh no*. The Ruijin's words suddenly returned to her and she started to struggle up.

"You need to get in touch with someone in Wiang. Gokan said that he hurt the female who helped me rent the summer house. That's how he knew where I was. You have to send help for her."

"Calm down, Jade," Inzen ordered, pulling her back against him.

"No! Don't you see? It's my fault that she was hurt. Someone has to go check on her." Weak tears trickled down her face at the thought of the delicate B'gento hurt by the brutish alien.

"She is already being cared for," Hrebec said. "She regained consciousness long enough to say that her attacker was searching for a human female. I am friends with one of the chief medics, so L'chong contacted me to warn me."

"Is she going to be all right?"

"He assured me that she will make a full recovery."

"Oh, thank God." More tears spilled down her cheeks, from relief this time, and Inzen's tail gently wiped them away. She snuggled into his arms, letting his comforting scent soothe her. She was half-asleep when they landed.

"Take her inside," Hrebec ordered. "Tell Abigail that I will fetch the medic and return."

Another quick trip through the rain and she was inside the house, warm and bright and full of the delicious smell of chocolate.

"Mama! Dada!" Lily came flying over as Inzen carried Jade into the kitchen and sat down with her on his lap.

Brown eyes opened wide as Lily put a gentle finger to the swollen flesh on her neck. "Mama hurt?"

"I'm fine, baby." She pushed against Inzen's arms until he reluctantly let her sit up enough so she could lean forward and hug their daughter. With a muttered exclamation, he lifted Lily onto his lap as well, and she sighed with contentment as Lily snuggled against them. "Daddy said you were a very brave girl."

"Brave," Lily agreed, then flashed her a wide, chocolate stained smile. "Got choclot."

"Well, not exactly. But close enough." Abby laughed. "Would you like some?"

"I'd love some."

A moment later, a warm mug was in her hands and she took a cautious sip. Mmm. As Abby said, it wasn't exactly chocolate and it had an odd, but not unpleasant, spicy aftertaste, but it was satisfyingly close. Lily wiggled down to join Tiana and Lucie, and Jade was half-asleep when Hrebec returned with the doctor. She was a thin Trevelorian female with an orange crest that reminded her of B'gento's but unlike the gentle property agent, she had a brusque, no-nonsense attitude.

"I'm Medic N'tana. And you are Jade?" Sharp yellow eyes surveyed her neck. "Looks like you have some swelling there. Any other injuries?"

"I'm fine—"

"She was shocked and unconscious for many minutes," Inzen interrupted. "She is not fine."

"I see." N'tana turned to Abby. "Is there a room I can use to examine her?"

"Of course. Let me show you to the guest room."

Jade started to try and stand, but Inzen simply rose with her in his arms.

"I can walk, you know," she muttered.

"Perhaps later. After the medic examines you."

"You Cire warriors." N'tana shook her head. "I'm glad that Trevelorian men are more reasonable in their approach."

"Oh, I don't know," Abby said as she led them into a small bedroom overlooking the village. "Didn't I see your mate telling that nice young teacher to stay away from you at the last festival?"

N'tana's beak-like nose turned bright red.

"I suspect L'vert had too much ale that day." The medic sighed. "But your point is well taken. All males are capable of irrational behavior. Now if you two will leave me alone with my patient…"

"I am not leaving," Inzen growled.

Abby laughed and whisked herself out of the room. "I'll leave you three to settle that one."

N'tana glared at Inzen, seemingly undeterred by the fact that he was twice her size. "My patient deserves privacy."

"My mate does not need privacy from me."

"Then why don't you put her down and let her speak for herself?"

He reluctantly placed her on the bed, his tail lingering on her wrist as he stood up. "Do you want me to leave, letari?"

Actually, she would probably have preferred to be alone with the medic, but he looked so anxious that she didn't have the heart to tell him to go. "No, it's fine if you stay."

N'tana snorted. "Fine. As long as he doesn't interfere."

"Why would I interfere?"

The medic ignored him and turned back to Jade. "Please remove your clothing."

"What? No!" Inzen roared.

Both of them looked at him, and he ducked his head. "I apologize. Do you want me to assist you, Jade?"

Well, yes, but this wasn't the time or place for that. Instead, she shook her head. "No, thanks."

"I will stand over here," he muttered, turning to look out the window. His shoulders were stiff with tension, his tail lashing anxiously.

As she started to undress, she regretted turning him down. Her muscles were tight and aching from the shock. N'tana stepped in as she fumbled with her shirt, her thin fingers cool and soothing as she helped Jade strip off her clothes and then bent closer to examine her neck injury.

"The damage to your neck is only superficial." N'tana smoothed a blue cream along the lines where the shock collar had been, and Jade felt an instant easing of the lingering soreness. Then the medic brought out a small scanner and ran it over her. "Your brainwaves are normal and your heart rhythm is stable. There should be no lingering effects from the shock. The stiffness in your muscles should go away with time but it would help to soak in a warm bath. I will leave some crystals for you to add to the water."

N'tana had been moving the scanner over her body as she spoke and she suddenly paused as she passed it over Jade's stomach.

"You were taken from your planet?" she said, frowning.

"That's right."

"How long ago?"

"I'm not really sure at this point. Maybe four weeks? Why?"

"Hmm." N'tana drew a sheet over her, then stood up and turned to face Inzen, still standing by the window. "I need to speak to your mate alone. This is not negotiable."

"Why? What is wrong?" He took a quick step towards the bed.

"Alone," N'tana repeated.

Jade's heart thudded against her chest. What had the medic found?

"Please, Inzen. Just for a minute," she whispered.

He gave her an agonized look, but he nodded. "I will be right outside the door. If you need anything, call for me."

As the door closed behind him, N'tana sighed and sat down on the bed next to her.

"I'm sorry about that, my dear, but I need to ask you some questions and I wasn't sure that he could handle the answers."

"What questions? You're scaring me."

N'tana's cool fingers closed around hers. "There is no need for fear. Whatever you decide, I will make sure that your wishes are obeyed."

"Decide about what?" she cried.

The medic hesitated. "I must ask, were you abused after you were taken?"

"You don't consider this abuse? It's the second time I've been shocked."

"Yes, of course, that is abuse, but I meant abuse of a sexual nature. Whatever you say will remain strictly between the two of us," she added when Jade stared at her. "While I don't recommend keeping secrets from each other, I understand that you may not wish your mate to know."

"No, there was nothing like that. I was lucky enough to be rescued before anything happened. Twice," she said with a shudder.

N'tana sat back, a relieved smile on her lips. "In that case, I hope this will be good news. My dear, you are with child."

Her ears rang. She must have misheard. "What? No, that's not possible."

"Why not?"

"I tried for so long on Earth. It took years to become pregnant with Lily. It can't have happened again." Despite her protests, a faint dizzying hope began to emerge. Her eyes filled with tears.

"I can assure you that it did." N'tana frowned at her. "You are unhappy? Because there are alternatives—"

"No! No, I'm not the least bit unhappy. Are you sure?"

"Very sure."

Joy filled her so completely that she felt as if she were floating. But she needed Inzen here to share in her happiness. "Inzen!"

He burst through the door so quickly he almost took it off its hinges. As he took in the tears now streaming down her face, he growled and advanced on N'tana.

"What have you done to her?"

"She hasn't done anything," Jade said quickly, holding out her hand to him. "I have the most wonderful news."

"What news?" Still eyeing N'tana suspiciously, he took her hand.

"We're going to have a baby!"

Her strong Cire warrior actually stumbled, collapsing to his knees next to the bed.

"A child?" he whispered.

"Yes. Isn't that wonderful?"

"But you said..."

"I know. Apparently, I was wrong." He was still staring at her, his face unreadable. "What's the matter? Aren't you happy?"

"Happy? Oh, my love."

He threw his arms around her waist and buried his head in her lap, his shoulders shaking. She heard the door close behind N'tana, but she was too busy running a soothing hand over Inzen's head to care.

"I never thought to be so blessed," he said when he finally raised his head. He laid a reverent hand over her stomach. "Another daughter."

"It could be a boy, you know."

"And I would be just as pleased with a son. But I think we will have a daughter. And her name will be Hana in honor of your grandmother."

"Thank you," she whispered.

The door opened and she looked up, expecting to see N'tana, but instead, a small brown head peeked around the corner.

"Mama sleep?"

"No, baby. Come join us."

She held out her hand and Lily flew across the room. Inzen lifted her onto the bed and then settled down with his arms around both of them, his tail curved protectively across Jade's stomach. Outside the rain continued to pour down but it didn't matter. The three of them were safe and warm and together.

It had taken being captured by aliens, but at last, she had the family she always wanted.

EPILOGUE

Twenty-one months later...

"Mama," Lily demanded as she came racing into the shop.

Jade put down the dress she'd been working on and smiled at her daughter. "What is it, baby?"

Lily came over and leaned against her side, her attention caught by the tiny garment. "Whatcha making?"

"A dress for Hana for her birthday." Her miraculous second daughter was turning one tomorrow. *Well, maybe not so miraculous*, she thought, her hand going to her stomach. She had snuck away for a visit to the medic this morning and the doctor confirmed Jade's suspicions: she was pregnant again. Her reproductive system apparently functioned just fine when a Cire male was involved. She couldn't wait to tell Inzen but for now, she hugged her secret to herself.

"It's pretty." Lily nodded approvingly as she studied the

dress with a critical eye. Jade already suspected that she would carry on the family tradition. Their daughter loved to spend time in the shop and had already learned some very basic stitches.

"Thank you," she said solemnly.

"Where's Auntie Cassie?" Lily asked.

"She's at the other shop."

After the terrible incident with the Ruijin, Cassie had finally started to make peace with her. She had actually agreed to Jade's suggestion about the shop window and began to listen to her marketing advice. Most of all, she had finally let her start sewing. By the time Hana was born, the two women were full partners. Six months ago, they opened a second location to satisfy the growing demand. Cassie wasn't quite young enough to be Jade's daughter, but she felt an almost maternal pride in watching the younger woman continue to find both her confidence and her peace of mind.

Lily fiddled with Jade's ring, her lip poking out. Inzen had bought the ring back and generously compensated B'hira for the loss of the pink flyer. Nothing could make up for the pain Gokan had caused B'gento, but the Trevelorian had assured Jade that she didn't blame her, and despite her lingering feeling of guilt, the two had become close friends.

Lily twirled the ring again and Jade hugged her closer.

"What's wrong, baby? Did you need me for something?"

"Dada won't let me play wif Hana."

Jade hid a smile. They had been concerned that Lily would be jealous, but from the beginning she demonstrated an almost proprietary interest in her sister and wanted to be involved in everything to do with her.

"Why not?"

"Nap time," Lily said gloomily. She had given up her

morning nap recently and didn't understand why Hana still took one.

"She needs her rest, baby. Remember that the two of you are spending the night with Auntie TeShawna tonight." Abby's long-ago prediction had come true. As soon as Jade and Cassie established a relationship, the other woman had come around.

"Yay!" Lily cheered, then gave her an anxious look. "Yous okay without us?"

Jade hid another smile. "Yes, baby. We'll be fine."

In fact, she had already made some definite plans for tonight, even before she found out the news. Inzen had been a little doubtful about letting the girls spend the night away from them, but she intended to take advantage of every minute.

As if her thoughts had conjured him up, he appeared in the doorway, Hana's tiny body tucked against one broad shoulder. Their daughter was a perfect mingling of the two of them. Her features were very like Jade's, but her skin was a pale green and she had a tiny, adorable tail.

"I thought it was nap time?" she asked, raising her eyebrow.

"So did I, but Bobo has gone missing again." Lily had ceremoniously presented Hana with the stuffed animal a month ago, and now they had a second daughter who wouldn't sleep without him. "The monitor says he is in here."

"Here he is!" Lily announced, pulling him out from under a pile of fabric and handing him to Hana who squealed happily.

"How in the world did he get there?" she asked.

"Perhaps he wanted to give me an excuse to kiss my beautiful mate." Inzen's eyes darkened as he bent over and brushed his mouth against hers, his tail curving around her waist. Even that small touch awakened her need for him, and her body responded.

"Yous kissing again," Lily said.

"Yes, we are," Inzen agreed as he straightened back up, his tail flicking teasingly across her now erect nipples. "Your mama needs a lot of kissing."

"Me too!"

"You too, little one." He scooped Lily up in his other arm and she kissed his cheek before nestling against him and patting Hana's back.

"Can you take them both back to the house? I want to finish Hana's dress today so I can give you all my attention tonight."

She deliberately licked her lips and saw his eyes darken again.

"I am very... eager for your attention."

"Tonight," she promised.

After Inzen left to take the girls to TeShawna's that evening, Jade hurried to their bedroom to prepare. With Hana's birth, they had decided they needed more room but rather than move away, Inzen bought the property behind them and added on to the house instead. *Just as well*, she thought, her hand caressing her stomach again.

Their new bedroom was larger and more spacious, but it still opened out to a private garden. She opened the doors to the garden, letting the sound of the fountain fill the room as she lit the small lanterns. The bedroom lights were already set to low and she undressed quickly, knowing he wouldn't be gone long. The silken rope went over a rafter, then she slipped her hands into the wrist loops, and waited, shivering with anticipation.

Inzen hurried back across the garden. He was still not entirely sure about leaving the girls for the night, but he intended to take full advantage of being alone with his mate.

She had been teasing him all afternoon with light touches and whispered promises. He threw open the door to their room and forgot how to breathe.

Jade was suspended from the rafters, her slender arms stretched above her head and her slim golden body glowing in the soft light. He stalked forward, noticing that her nipples were already taut with excitement and the heady scent of her arousal mixed with her natural sweet, spicy fragrance. She was completely naked except for a sparkling green stone suspended between her breasts. After everything that had happened, the idea of a mating bracelet no longer had the same appeal. Instead, they had agreed to put the jewels aside for the girls—all except for one perfect stone, which he had made into this necklace.

She wore it constantly, usually hidden beneath her clothes, but he liked knowing that she wore a symbol of their joining. He traced a finger along the thin gold chain, lingering between her breasts as he circled the stone, and saw her shiver.

"I like you clad only in this."

"I know you do." Her gaze flicked down to where his cock was straining at his pants. "And I like you clad in nothing at all."

He quickly stripped away his clothes, and returned to her, his shaft a heated bar between them as his tail circled her waist and pulled her closer. Her hands were still stretched above her head, and he ran his hand up them until he found a silken cord circling her wrists and leading up to the rafters. Some primitive instinct roared approval at the idea of her bound for his pleasure.

"What is this?"

"I said something once about you leaving me hanging. You thought I meant it literally and I... liked the idea." She grasped the cord above her wrists and lifted her weight, spinning in a slow circle so he could admire all of her delightful body.

"Hmm, I can see the advantages. I can tease these impudent little nipples." He bent his head and sucked a taut bud deep into his mouth. "Or fill my hands with your luscious little ass." He spun her around, then lifted her easily to kiss a line between her quivering cheeks.

Since she was already at the perfect height, he spun her again and pressed his mouth to her delicious cunt. He groaned as her sweet taste flooded his mouth. Her body arched backwards, opening her even more to his touch and he focused on the hard little nub of her pleasure receptacle, bringing her to a quick, hard climax.

Oh, yes, he definitely approved of this idea of hers.

As her shudders died away, he drew her back down his body until she was perched just above the straining head of his cock. He rubbed her slowly back and forth along the thick nubbed length, prolonging both their pleasure.

"Inzen, please."

At her whispered plea, he brought her down over his cock in one long, hard stroke. She cried out and once again arched backwards, her body in a taut, beautiful line. He bent forward, his hand supporting her as he enclosed her breast in his mouth, licking and sucking the quivering flesh as he began a slow, rocking rhythm, letting her swing out and back on his cock. His tail circled beneath her, probing gently, before finally slipping inside her bottom hole. The additional tightness sent a shock of pleasure through his system, and he could feel her quivering, on the verge of climax. His patience deserted him and he abandoned his leisurely pace, thrusting with mindless desire as she convulsed around him. Fire raced down his spine and the base of his cock expanded, impossibly tight now, as his release swept over him and he called out her name, clinging to her with desperate hands as he exploded deep inside her.

With the last of his strength, he carried her to the bed and collapsed, their bodies still locked together and his heart full.

"I have something to tell you," his mate whispered a few minutes later and he tried to force aside the lazy contentment filling him to focus on her.

"What is that, my love? You are opening a third location?"

She laughed. "Well, I've been thinking about it, but I think I'm going to wait for another year. I think I'm going to be rather busy."

"Yes?" he asked absently, his hand curving around her breast. When she laughed, they bounced most delightfully.

"I'm going to be busy because—oh!"

She gasped as he pulled gently on the taut little bud of her nipple, bigger and darker now than when they had met. Unable to resist, he lowered his head to taste the tempting morsel of flesh and she moaned. His barely softened cock jerked as her snug little cunt tightened around him when he increased the pressure. *So sensitive*, he thought approvingly. She was always responsive to his touch, but she hadn't been this sensitive since...

A sudden wild hope beat in his heart, and he lifted his head. "What did you want to tell me?"

"Later," she said, trying to tug his head back down. "That feels so good."

"I will make it feel even better," he promised. "After you tell me."

Her face lit up and he knew he had guessed correctly even before she spoke.

"We're going to have another baby."

Even though he had thought himself drained, his cock was

once again fully erect and he saw her eyes widen before she smiled up at him.

"I can tell you like the idea."

"I love the idea that you are pregnant with my child," he said firmly as his hips gave an involuntary thrust forward and they both moaned.

"Good. Then about your promise to make me feel even better…"

"A Cire warrior always fulfills a promise," he agreed, and proceeded to do just that.

Afterwards, they lay curled together in contented silence. Only one doubt marred his happiness. Although she seemed to handle the shop and their daughters—and him—with effortless ease, his instincts demanded that he protect her. Her small body was so delicate compared to his.

"I am concerned that this pregnancy will be too much for you. You do so much already."

"Don't worry. I'll be fine."

"Perhaps we should hire additional help."

"We can if we need to, but I'm not worried about it. I have a good team working for me, I've got the support of our friends and family, and most of all, I have you." Her hand reached up and cupped his cheek, her face so full of love that his heart ached. "You have given me everything I ever wanted."

"As have you." She had given him love, hope, and a second chance for a family. "I love you, my letari."

"I love you too."

She yawned and snuggled closer. He wrapped his arms around her as they drifted off to sleep to the gentle sounds of the fountain in their new house, in the new world they had built, together.

AUTHORS' NOTE

Thank you for reading **Daughter of the Alien Warrior**! We had an amazing time giving another Cire Warrior and his human mate a chance to find love, family, and their happily ever after! Inzen is a male who lost – and gained - so much, and it is no coincidence that we've released his story on Father's Day.

The *Treasured by the Alien* series would not be possible without the involvement of these wonderful people...

To our fantastic readers: Your love of this series simply blows us away! Another Cire is going to find his mate and family because of your incredible support.

To our awesome beta readers and our proofreader, Janet S, Nancy V, and Kitty S: Thank you for giving our book your time and valuable feedback. As always, you ladies rock!

To our fabulous cover designers, Naomi Lucas and Cameron Kamenicky: We requested 'a cute baby cover' and you replied, 'We got this.' Know what? You absolutely delivered. Baby Lily is gushingly adorable!

AUTHORS' NOTE

To our loving families: You provide us with unending inspiration and support. We love you all dearly.

Again, thank you for reading our book! Whether you enjoyed the story or not, it would mean the world to us if you left an honest review at Amazon. Reviews help other readers find books to enjoy, which helps the authors as well!

All the best,
Honey & Bex

If you'd like to know more about what's happening in our worlds, please visit our websites!

www.honeyphillips.com
www.bexmclynn.com

OTHER TITLES

Treasured by the Alien

by Honey Phillips and Bex Mclynn

Mama and the Alien Warrior

A Son for the Alien Warrior

Daughter of the Alien Warrior

Cosmic Fairy Tales

The Ugly Dukeling by Bex McLynn

Jackie and the Giant by Honey Phillips

Books by Honey Phillips

The Alien Abduction Series

Anna and the Alien

Beth and the Barbarian

Cam and the Conqueror

Deb and the Demon

Ella and the Emperor

Faith and the Fighter

Greta and the Gargoyle

Hanna and the Hitman

The Alien Invasion Series

Alien Selection

Alien Conquest

Alien Prisoner

Alien Breeder

Alien Alliance

Alien Hope

Cyborgs on Mars

High Plains Cyborg

The Good, the Bad, and the Cyborg

A Fistful of Cyborg

A Few Cyborgs More

The Magnificent Cyborg

Books by Bex McLynn

The Ladyships Series

Sarda

Thanemonger

Bane

Standalone

Rein: A Tidefall Novel

Printed in Great Britain
by Amazon